# SOMEDAY...

I doze off and on, off and on, but don't really get into a hard sleep. Finally I'm just awake. I wish Jackie would come in and talk to me. But she went home.

Lonely here.

Lonely...

Someday I will never be lonely. I'll make sure of that. No basements, no hospital rooms. Living upstairs with my parents, eating dinner with them. And when I'm grown up, I'll jog like Father does. Go outside. Jog in the rain. Three, five times a day. All day. Just to feel that wide, forever openness. No walls at all. Maybe I'll live outside. When I'm grown up.

Outside... that's what got me into trouble.

"Shaw's tight writing style and suspenseful story line make the book difficult to put down, and its realistic nature draws the reader in and makes one want Charlie to succeed."
                                                                —*VOYA*

# THE BOY FROM

# THE BASEMENT

## SUSAN SHAW

**speak**

An Imprint of Penguin Group (USA) Inc.

SPEAK

Published by the Penguin Group

Penguin Group (USA) Inc., 345 Hudson Street, New York, New York 10014, U.S.A.

Penguin Group (Canada), 90 Eglinton Avenue East, Suite 700, Toronto, Ontario, Canada M4P 2Y3
(a division of Pearson Penguin Canada Inc.)

Penguin Books Ltd, 80 Strand, London WC2R 0RL, England

Penguin Ireland, 25 St Stephen's Green, Dublin 2, Ireland (a division of Penguin Books Ltd)

Penguin Group (Australia), 250 Camberwell Road, Camberwell, Victoria 3124, Australia
(a division of Pearson Australia Group Pty Ltd)

Penguin Books India Pvt Ltd, 11 Community Centre, Panchsheel Park, New Delhi - 110 017, India

Penguin Group (NZ), Cnr Airborne and Rosedale Roads, Albany, Auckland 1310, New Zealand
(a division of Pearson New Zealand Ltd)

Penguin Books (South Africa) (Pty) Ltd, 24 Sturdee Avenue, Rosebank,
Johannesburg 2196, South Africa

Registered Offices: Penguin Books Ltd, 80 Strand, London WC2R 0RL, England

First published in the United States of America by Dutton Children's Books,
a division of Penguin Young Readers Group, 2004
Published by Speak, an imprint of Penguin Group (USA) Inc., 2006

10 9 8 7 6 5 4 3 2 1

CIP Data is available.

Speak ISBN 0-14-240546-9

Designed by Heather Wood

Printed in the United States of America

## ACKNOWLEDGMENTS

Many thanks to Martha Fenoglio, Terry VanHook, Jean Soule, Doris Markley, and Eileen Spinelli for their insightful comments on the manuscript and for their treasured friendship.

Also a huge thank-you to my editor, Julie Strauss-Gabel, who helped me bring out the best in Charlie's story, and to Margaret E. Blaustein, Ph.D., whose contributions from her perspective as a mental-health professional were invaluable.

And, of course, bouquets to my husband, John, and our children, Janet, Ben, and Warren, for all their support.

*To my parents,*
    *David and Jean Wetherill,*
        *with great, great love*

# THE BOY
## FROM THE
### BASEMENT

# PART ONE

# CHAPTER ONE

I'm sitting in a basement smelling of old, burned furnace oil. Empty and raw, no feeling of ease or well-being. Just being. The floor is brown, flaking linoleum, cold to my legs below my shorts. It's dusty. No shirt, and the shorts—Father's old ones—don't fit. I am alone down here.

My shoulder aches, and I'm hungry. I lean against the bottom step of the basement, waiting for my parents to go to bed. Maybe there will be food.

*Click!* as Father unlocks the basement door, but I don't move. Not yet.

The steps to the second floor creak as my parents climb up to bed. My mother answers something my father says. I wait through the shower and the toilet flushes. I wait until all is still and creep softly up to the door. I open it.

As usual it is dark in the kitchen except for what comes in from the streetlight. I open the bread drawer. Something's left in there. I pull it out, leaving the drawer open. I check to make sure there's more than a couple of slices. It can't look like I've taken anything. Then I remove a knife from the drainer and use it to spread peanut butter thickly on my hand-held slice before eating over the sink. I don't linger over the food, but I thrill to the stickiness filling my mouth.

Oh, food! It tastes so good, and my whole body hums as the sandwich trails down to my stomach. Between bites I tilt my head beneath the chained cabinets for long drinks from a thin, silent stream of water from the faucet. Upstairs, they can't be allowed to hear anything. Then I wash the knife under the same stream. I silently replace it in the drainer and put the bread back into the drawer. Close it.

I check the bathroom off the kitchen. Locked. As usual.

Then I do the riskiest thing. I open the back door and stand in the cold blackness of the little back porch to pee onto the grass. No one will see, and I can't go in the basement anywhere.

Sometimes the b.m.'s force me out into the backyard. I bunch my towel into a doorstop, then leave the porch for a spot in the darkness behind the pine trees. Father never goes back there, so it's all right. Someday, when the punishment is over, I'll take a shovel through the yard and bury it all. In the meantime, I hope for hard rain.

Tonight it's just pee. There is no breeze to shut the door behind me, but I hold it with one hand just in case. My bladder shrinks. Oh! Relief!

I stand for only a few seconds, the night air crisp on my skin. Outside—where the wind and rain run free—but I keep my hand tight on the door. Tightly, I also hold down my wish to be as free as the wind.

Then back inside, pull the door shut—*Click!*—and I'm tiptoeing down the basement steps again. Made it through one more day.

# CHAPTER TWO

I wake in the morning with the *tramp-tramp*ing on the kitchen floor overhead. I imagine my father eating his oatmeal, my mother stirring her coffee. I smell the coffee, hear the *Clink, clink!* of teaspoon against china. White china with one pink flower on the cup.

No other sounds. My parents don't say much in the morning—an occasional word, maybe.

*Slam!* from the front door. Father's gone for his morning jog.

"Charlie?" Mother calls through the basement door. Father's locked it by now. "Are you making it?"

I cough before I speak. "I'm making it."

"There's an apple behind the cookbooks," she says.

"Thanks."

There's a pause, but I know she hasn't moved.

"Charlie?"

"Yes?"

"I'm so sorry."

"I know."

"Someday, Charlie."

Father's key clicks in the front door. He must have only made a run to the mailbox at the corner. Mother's footsteps hurry—tile to carpet—to the computer in the dining room. She's at work now.

I lie still under the old towel I stole from the bottom of the linen closet when I knew no one was home. That was before lock-ins. Father wouldn't miss the towel, and I had to have something. The basement is cold.

I wonder how Mother managed to keep the apple for me with Father always counting everything. An apple. I haven't tasted one for a while. The last thing Mother saved for me was an onion. Boy, did it taste good! But an apple . . . my mouth waters.

Used to be Mother brought down food and juice when Father went jogging, but twice he caught her. Then there was the third time—*Quick! Up the steps!*—when we heard his key in the door. She just made it.

He must have known, though, because that was the end of it. Now, the door is locked all day. "You OK, Charlie?" "I'm OK, Mother" is about all we can do now. But there is usually peanut butter, and it always tastes wonderful.

Staircase creaking under Father's feet. The creaks are loudest when he's the one going up. They creak a little under Mother, and when they're both going up at once, it sounds like something coming loose. I can do it with no creaking. Or, at least, I could. I haven't been on those steps in a long time.

The shower comes on, and Father's singing voice travels down to me through the running water. I like his singing. It means he feels good. Maybe he feels good enough to end the punishment and call me upstairs.

The staircase creaks again. A couple of words I don't understand rumble to Mother as Father walks through the dining room. A soft answer from her, the scuff of footsteps from the carpet to the kitchen tiles, and Father's at his desk. Right on the other side of the door at the top of the basement steps. An invisible but uncuttable line attached to him pulls on my chest. I crawl up the steps and touch the door. He must know I'm here.

I want to call him. Father! Do you feel me like I feel you? Is it hard for you to work knowing there's only a door between us? You would see me if you opened it. True and real. You could hear me breathe like I hear you—if you tried. Is it hard not to open the door and say, "Charlie, come on up!"

It has to be as hard for him as it is for me. So I don't call. I crawl down again—silently. I have to wait until he says it's time. That's what he told me. I have learned to believe what he says.

I sit back on the floor, lean against the bottom step. The spider on the ceiling above me spins her web. How she takes her time! After all, why hurry? She's not going anywhere. As long as she doesn't weave a web to catch me—that idea always lurks in the back of my mind. On my good days, I know I'm too big for her to want, but still I worry. As long as she has smaller things to catch, I'm all right.

She swells up while I look, then flattens down again so I can hardly see her. How did she do that? I watch to see if she'll do it again, but she doesn't. Then right as I turn my head, I see her puff up once more out of the corner of my eye. When I turn my head, though, it's like nothing happened. The spider taunts me with her sameness. I watch a long time this time, but she doesn't move at all.

I hear the leaves shifting under the wind, losing myself in the rolling, *shhshh*ing sound.

I pick up my pencils from behind the steps. Mother sticks them under the door once in a while. Sharpens them for me sometimes. There's paper behind the steps, too—old computer paper left by the people who lived here before. Stacks of it.

I feel the ridges in the wood of a pencil, touch the marks stamped in the yellow paint, let the blackness transfer from the point and stain my fingertips. Then I slide a paper into a patch of sunlight trapped by the window well and draw. I've drawn everything in the basement over and over—the furnace, the water heater, the old red wagon with two wheels missing, and the gray clothesline still dotted with clothespins. All from the people who lived here before us.

I feel myself at the kitchen table when I draw, and it's the way things used to be. I'm *there*. Mother and Father work, and I draw—*there*. But when the drawing ends, the table goes, and I am still, still here.

Today I draw random lines without thinking too much about what it is. Like the spider, I'm in no hurry. There's plenty of time.

But right now I don't feel like drawing. I'm tired of the endless stretch of time. I've been down here so long, and I don't feel real good. When is Father going to let me upstairs again? When will my punishment be over?

Was what I did this bad?

I drop my pencil and roll onto my back. I'm sick of drawing. The spider's up on the ceiling, as always. Dark red with black markings like two bent fingers facing each other. And a bunch of black legs busy, always busy. The spider's head turns to look down. Father's face bulges out at me. I blink. No. It's only the spider. Father's upstairs, of course. What made my eyes play that trick?

After I lie here for a while, I begin to shiver. I'm colder suddenly. I pull the towel around me. Then I'm too hot, sweating, even. I blot my sweat with the towel, but that takes too much energy. So I just sweat, feeling the gathering liquid drip onto the floor. I'm cold again.

What's happening? I can't be sick. Can't. There's no extra energy for that. Only for just making it through the day.

Drowsiness creeps over me, and my body feels heavy, ready to sink into the floor. I gladly give in to sleep, the sweetest time taker. . . .

I wake up, holding onto the shield of sleep until I can no longer pretend. I'm still sick, and the presence of the spider and her web is strong. She's going to get me, and I'm afraid, so afraid.

Sick with a terrible thirst and scared, scared.

Calm, Charlie—stay calm. No energy to be upset. Don't have any to waste.

I lie still and wait. Upstairs, a clock chimes. I count four. Count five. Count six.

# CHAPTER THREE

Dark again. My parents are in the kitchen. The radio is on.

If I came upstairs, would they help me? Father doesn't want the spider to eat me, does he? I'm being punished is all. Someday Father will open the door and call down, "Come on up, Charlie. Punishment's over."

Maybe the punishment's over already, and they're about to call me upstairs. Then food, a hot shower, a soft bed, my father's jokes, my mother's smiles. Like it used to be. Didn't it?

"Mother," I croak out. "Father."

But my voice won't work, and they don't hear me over the radio. I haven't used my voice much in so long, and it hurts my stomach to try. In a way, I'm glad they don't hear me.

Another day I opened the kitchen door when they were still up. That was before lock-ins, before I stopped being so scared all the time. I couldn't stand being down here. I was so lonely and hungry. Mother and Father were having dinner— meat loaf and baked potatoes steaming right there in front of me. They looked up at the opening door.

"Can I live upstairs again, please? I'm really sorry for what I did." I was, too, and I could almost taste that hot food, three steps away.

My mother looked at my father. I could see she wanted to say yes. But Father makes the decisions.

He said, "Charlie, I was just about to tell you you're allowed out of the basement, but I can't now. You have to wait until I say it." And his voice was sad. I'd disappointed him again.

"Oh, Charlie." Just above a whisper. Mother's face was pale, her napkin next to her plate. But she could do nothing. I knew that.

"Eat your food, Trish," my father said to Mother. She picked up her fork and put a small amount of meat loaf into her mouth while Father watched. Then he said, "Go on back down, Charlie. You're upsetting your mother."

She shook her head at me—short, quick shakes—while Father's eyes were on me. A message: it's not your fault.

But it was.

"Sorry, Mother," I said, before closing the door again.

Down I went. How long? How long? I wondered. I still wonder. That was so long ago. If Father was almost ready to call me that day, why am I still down here? I don't understand.

So I wait, as usual, for them to go up to bed. Waiting—a blank, silent emptiness that fills time like a small cloud growing to fill the sky.

When the house is quiet, I crawl up the steps, but I hold on to my towel. That will be my weapon against the spider.

My stomach hurts, so I skip the food. Sometimes there's not enough bread or there's no peanut butter, so it's not the first time. I'll get the apple on the way down. Eat it later. Water—I drink from the tap, a long drink. So dry, so dry. But then I begin to sweat again.

I try to turn the water off, but the spigot won't go all the way, and I really have to pee.

I'll turn that off when I come back inside.

Outside, I stand on the porch. A steady breeze cools my damp head. I grip the door to steady my legs. I'm not ready, but my bladder lets go, anyway. Panicked, I drop my hand from the door to crouch, to wipe the floor with the towel. Father can't see my pee on the porch. Then he'll know—

*CRASH!*

The door slams shut in a gust of wind, echoing between the houses. Oh, no! My parents have to hear that. I go to a fear so quiet and complete that it's almost a solid wall around me. How can fear be so quiet?

My hurting gut won't let me stand straight, but I stand. The wind lifts again. Hair blows in my face while, bent over, I try the door. I have to get in, I must get in, to turn off the water and go back to the basement before my parents come downstairs. I turn the knob and pull on it, but it won't give.

Locked.

Of course.

I knew that.

I stand in my father's old, peed-in shorts, my feet in cold pee puddled on the porch floor. All is silence, except for the wind in the leaves and the hair blown across my eyes. I turn my head, and the wind whips my hair away, drying new sweat.

No light comes on inside the house, no voices, nothing.

What can I do?

Then I see the spider. She's big now, as big as I am, and

she's right by the door. How she got here, I don't know. I take a swipe at her with my towel and run down the steps. Except I can't run, and I fall into the grass. The grass is soft and wet. It cools my sweaty, hot body. Feels good. But I can't stay in it because the spider will get me.

My stomach hurts so much, but I make myself get up. I have to get away from the spider. I have to get back in the basement, too. How can I do both? The spider's between me and the house. Crunched over, I make it through the wet grass to the sidewalk underneath the streetlight. I'm cold, but the water on the grass makes my feet colder. Under the streetlight I don't see the spider, so I sit on the curb with my feet in the gravelly street. Everything—the curb, the street, the wind—is cold. I am cold all through.

The light blinks off. Scared, I stare up at the darkness where the light was, willing it to come on again, but it doesn't. I can't see the spider, but her rasping breath— *Ihmm!-Ihmm!*—laces through the wind's roar.

Afraid, I stand up. Which way, which way?

*Sting! Sting! Sting!* Her legs burn my back!

Panicked, I swing the towel where I know she is. "Get off, get off, get off!"

Still bent over, I try to run, but it's more of a hobbled walk. Another streetlight way far away promises me safety, and that's the path I take, smacking at the spider with the towel every time I feel her hot breath. Can't let her touch me again. She'll kill me!

Another kind of roar takes over, and lights are everywhere. Can't see.

*ErrRRR-HO-ONNK!! SCREE-EECH!* A car headlight stops so close I can reach it with my hand. It feels smooth in its whiteness.

"Dumb kid!" someone shouts. "Get outta the road!"

The car zags around me and disappears, leaving me in darkness again.

It is bad out here. Father's right.

On and on to the safety of the streetlight. Finally, I'm in its circle of light. Safe. As long as I'm in the circle, the spider won't get me. I know this, and I sit on the curb.

"Hhh . . ." I sigh and my head drops to my knees. OK for now.

But the basement—it's far away now. How will I get back to it with the spider waiting just outside the light?

I shiver again and wrap the towel around me. It's not too wet, and I breathe with my mouth open so I won't smell the pee.

The basement—the spider—the basement—the spider—

# CHAPTER FOUR

"It's OK, honey; we'll get you all fixed up."

Who's that?

Something touches my arms and legs and I feel myself rise. Weightless. I open my eyes. People all around me. People I don't know.

Where's the spider?

But I shake my head. Too hard to talk, and I'm dizzy.

Then I realize. The basement. I have to get back before—

I struggle to get free.

Water's running in the kitchen, and pee's on the porch floor. I'm afraid.

"Take it easy, honey. You're OK."

Shivering again. But why? I don't feel cold. I want my towel, but it's disappeared. A blanket drops somehow to cover me. So soft, so warm, it must be dark green. But the basement—

Wait. I'm inside my father's car. The engine is running. Did he find me? It must be so.

"Father?" Where's he taking me?

"No, honey." It's the same voice. "I'm Ellie. What happened to you? Why were you lying there?"

I don't tell her about the spider. As long as I don't say it, that keeps her away. Instead I say, "Because of the light." There. Ellie will understand what that means. "Because of the light." I don't have to mention the spider.

Ellie raises her eyebrows in the half shadows. I don't get why.

I'm worried about the basement, but I can't help it. The blanket is so warm and soft, and I feel so bad, I burrow down into it to fall in and out of sleep to the low hum of the motorrrr . . .

. . . stop.

"We're taking you inside," says Ellie. "This is where you belong."

But I watch while they carry me. It's not the basement. It's a big building with bright lights. How come I belong here now, instead of the basement? My father sent me because of the pee and the running water? That must be it. But what is this place?

Bright lights, changing faces. People talking high, fast, and loud. I can't focus on any of it. I'm hot and cold at the same time. I need something to hold on to, need things to stop moving.

"Father?" I call. "Mother?" Or at least, I think I do.

Then everything twists faster and faster until darkness falls over it all.

---

I wake up. The basement floor feels different. The light is coming from the wrong place. There's too much of it, and it hurts my eyes. What happened to the basement? Did I fall asleep in a funny corner?

But the ceiling looks different, too. Clean and white and no spider overhead. That's where the light starts, too, from a fixture in the crook between the wall and the ceiling. There was never a light there before. Underneath it is a window, but it's not in the window well. Through the window, it's dark, still night outside.

Oh! Where's the spider? That's important. I sit up fast. Dizziness. Then it fades.

A bed! What am I doing in a bed? I'm not supposed to sleep in a bed. That's part of the punishment. So I'll appreciate what I have and not be going where I'm not supposed to go.

*But no one saw me.*

*You better learn to listen.*

What's wrong? Where am I? This isn't the basement. Father will be angry with me for leaving the basement. Oh, I remember. I was bad. I peed on the porch and left the water on. So Father sent me here.

I am right. He is angry. But what is here?

I lie back down. My heart's beating fast. Scared. Where am I? How can I go home? How can I find out?

Calm, Charlie, calm. Think of something else. OK, the bed. Think of beds, warm and soft.

I had a bed at the lake house. It had a wooden headboard and a blanket. A dark green one, so soft against my cheek. A pillow, too, just like this one, and a bed table for my glass of water. And there was a small, round rug on the floor where I'd set my feet when I got up. Braided, it was, all gold and brown and warm when the morning sun streaked across it. I could see the lake through the window when I stood on it. I have that bed at the basement house, too, at least I think I still do, but the lake isn't where I can see it from that bedroom. I miss the lake. I miss the cry of the loon.

I touch the clean sheets, the pale yellow blanket. I'm clean, too. My hands are pink instead of that gray I got used to. That's good. But how come I don't remember getting clean?

I wiggle my toes where I can't see them. A bed. I'm scared, but this bed sure feels good.

Why am I in a bed? What is this place, and how can this be punishment?

Did I die? No. I'm still breathing. That means I'm alive, right?

There's a cord attached to my arm from something that looks like a coatrack on wheels. Father knows I don't run away. Why did he tie me up? He knows I'll wait for him.

I look on the other side of the bed where it's not so bright.

The spider! She's gonna get me!

I push the covers back and stand up quick. Dizzy, and the sweats start again. I prop myself against the bed until my head steadies. I look back at the spider. Better hurry. She's coming. I push the coatrack thing and run with it into a big hall. I slow down, dizzy again, but I keep on. One foot in front of the other, one foot in front of the other, into half darkness.

"Whoa, there." Mother has my elbow. Must be Mother. "You need something?" But her voice is funny, like maybe she has a cold.

I look behind me. I don't see the spider, but she's there. I can feel her.

"What's the matter?"

"I-I don't know." But the words trail into the fading hall.

Mother steers my wobbly legs quickly back to the room. "Into bed with you," she says.

She arranges the covers over me again and I lie with my eyes closed while the room settles around me. When I open my eyes again, Mother's gone. There's another lady in the room with me, and she's wearing white. The spider is back in her corner, waiting, watching.

"OK, now?" The lady holds my wrist gently in her hand and looks at her watch. "I'm Dee."

"Where's Mother?"

"I don't know."

"But she was just here." I sit up to look. She has to be here.

"No, honey. That was me the whole time."

Mother's not here? Dee does have that cold-y voice. But I don't know Dee. Why did Father send me to be with Dee?

"You go back to sleep now, honey," says Dee. "Maybe your mama will be here when you wake up."

My mama? What's that?

But Dee leaves the room before I can ask her.

# CHAPTER FIVE

Something wakes me up. Outside the window, the night sky is touched with brightness, and there's a man bending over my bed. Afraid, I pull away to the other side of the bed. Who is this man? Why is he here?

The man smiles, squinting at me through his glasses. "Hi. My name's Doc Patel." His voice is high and light. "All right if I check you over?"

I don't answer, wishing myself invisible. The cord from the coatrack tugs against my arm, and the blanket confines my feet. I can't get away. The man is watching me. What does he want? He doesn't look angry, but you can't tell from that every time.

"I'm a doctor," he says slowly, the high voice deepening. "I'm here to help you."

What would Father say? I got checked over by a doctor that time at the lake house. It was all right with Father that time, and if Father sent me here . . .

I nod, but I don't say anything. Best not to say anything.

"What's your name?"

I shrug that off, forgetting—Ouch!—my bad shoulder. But then it's better, like always. Why does Doc Patel ask me my name? He has to know it if Father sent me here.

But where is Father?

"Your shoulder hurt?" the doctor asks.

"No."

I try not to notice the pain while Doc Patel moves my bad arm around. Instead I picture Father walking the early morning streets, looking for me, waving a flashlight from side to side. *Charlie,* he calls, but softly, so no one else hears. It's important that nobody else hears. *Charlie! Where are you?* If they see you, they can get you! *Charlie!* I wish I was there to answer.

But Father wouldn't be searching for me. He knows where I am because he sent me here. Father will be coming into this room soon to see me here. To see if the punishment can be over.

Doc Patel listens to my chest and back through a funny-looking black thing. "It's called a stethoscope," he explains, even though I don't ask. "How are you feeling?"

I pause before answering. "I don't know."

"You've got a nasty fever," he says, "but we'll take care of it."

"What's wrong with me?"

"An infection. But we'll knock it out, and you'll be back riding your bike in no time."

My bike? I don't have a bike. Bikes are for wild kids. That's what Father says. Kids whose parents don't care about them and let them go outside whenever they want. I don't want a bike. Not like the girl who used to live across the street. Boy, could she ride!

Doc Patel leaves, and my mind drifts back and forth. Sometimes I'm asleep; sometimes I'm not. It all feels pretty much the same. And always hot.

Awake.

A bed? What?! Oh, right.

I want to go home. To the basement. That's where I need to be. With the window well, the two-wheeled wagon. The steps to the kitchen where I hear my parents together. The smell of coffee. The chance of living upstairs again. If I could, I'd wrap those crumbling basement walls around me

*Clip-clunk! Clip-clunk!* A tall, tall lady with noisy shoes comes into my room. I look at her feet. Red. My mother doesn't wear red shoes. I didn't know anyone did. Her shoes make my eyes hurt way into my head.

"Hi," she says, and sits down on a chair by my bed.

Why is she here? I'm not supposed to see people. That's what Father says. Or, at least, they're not supposed to see me.

"My name's Dr. Leidy." My head slowly pounds around her words. "I'm a psychologist. That means I help people feel better inside their heads and help them answer questions about what bothers them."

I don't understand what she's talking about.

"What's your name?"

She shouldn't be talking to me. That's against the rules. But she found me. I wonder if that will make a difference when Father asks. Either way, I don't want to talk to her with my head hurting and hurting and hurting.

"We don't know your name," says Dr. Leidy.

So? You're not supposed to know it. You're not supposed to

see me. I'm invisible. Why does this lady have to talk to me when my head hurts? She has to already know my name since my parents sent me here.

Maybe this is a test. Like the spider. I'm getting used to the spider. Same as I got used to my shoulder hurting. Maybe I have to get used to my head hurting, too.

Anyway, my name's Charlie. I know that. She knows that. So that must not be the answer. Maybe I'm not supposed to answer. Maybe I'm supposed to know something else. Which is it?

I look at Dr. Leidy. She smiles and waits. She and the spider both wait.

Here goes.

"Charlie," I say, and cringe against the smack. *I told you not to speak! But—But nothing!* There is no smack.

"Are you afraid, Charlie?"

I look at Dr. Leidy. She hasn't moved. Her gray eyes are steady on mine. I'm not sure I like that. I look away to the spider. She's getting darker. Her legs move all around her body.

"No," I say. Can't ever say you're afraid. But I am. All the time.

"You're safe here, Charlie. No one's going to hurt you."

Except the spider. OK, I'm not thinking about the spider. She's just there in her web. Like the window is there. Not the window well.

"What's your last name?"

Last name? This one I don't know at all. What's that mean? The name I had before it was Charlie?

Dr. Leidy turns her head sideways to look at me.

"Do you know your last name?"

Did I ever have another name? I must have. But what is it? Charlie's the only name I remember.

"Charlie." That's what I say.

Dr. Leidy writes something on a brown clipboard. Father has a clipboard, but his is black. I wonder what Dr. Leidy writes. Was my answer OK? I can't tell by her face.

"I'm writing things down so I don't forget them, Charlie," she says to me. "Do you know your phone number?"

"My head hurts." I push my hand against the *pound-pound-pound!*

"I'm sorry, Charlie. I have to ask these questions. I'll stop soon."

I shrug my good side and look away, still pushing against my head. *Pound, pound, pound!*

"What's your telephone number?"

"Telephone number?" But there is no number. Just a telephone. "We don't have a telephone *number*."

"All right. Where do you live?"

I look around the room, avoiding the spider's corner. Isn't this where I live now? It's where I am. It's where I'm supposed to be. That's what the lady, Ellie, said. So I live here. Not the basement.

"Here?" Is that what she wants?

Dr. Leidy puts down her clipboard.

"Charlie. This is King's Hospital. No one lives here. It's a place for sick people."

"Oh. Well . . ."

"Last night the police found you sleeping outside—almost in the street. The police brought you here."

Police? Ellie was the police? She wasn't like the police I remember from the lake house. That one was a man with a real deep voice. I could tell by his voice that he liked to laugh, but he wasn't laughing when my father was talking to him. He wasn't laughing while he talked to me. I kind of wished he would. I wished everybody would stop looking so upset and laugh. Then we could be happy again.

Dr. Leidy keeps talking. "No one knows who you are. If you tell us, that will help us get you to a safe place."

"Back with my parents, you mean? But they sent me here. In my father's car. Besides, I told you. I'm Charlie. That's who I am."

A shadow falls from the doorway.

"Dr. Leidy?" It's a man's voice. I'm glad he doesn't come into the room. His shadow is so big, and his voice is so low.

"Just a minute." Dr. Leidy leaves her seat to talk to the man in the hallway. His voice rumbles like Father's, but it's not Father's. I can catch some of his words, but I don't care at first. Then I know he and Dr. Leidy are talking about me.

"Terrible thing . . . nobody's seen him there . . . terrible . . . parents . . . shoulder . . . abandoned?"

They think my parents are terrible. But they aren't. I love my parents, and I know they love me. I'm bad, that's all. I'm being punished, but my parents would never hurt me. Well, my shoulder—that was an accident. Father didn't mean to throw me so hard against the wall. He said so. Well, I know he meant to say so, but I couldn't help crying at first—*Stop that noise!*—and he really hates it when people cry. When I cry. So I—so I held it down. I made myself stop. By then, he'd left the house to walk. That's what I make him do—walk and walk and walk when I mess up.

After he'd left, Mother touched my shoulder. "Are you all right, Charlie?" and I gasped, backing away.

"I'll go lie down," I said, through the white-lightning jabs of pain. "It will be better soon."

Because I didn't want to worry her any more than she was. There was nothing she could do.

"I'm so sorry, Charlie."

"I know."

"Someday it will be better. I promise."

"Sure." And I believed her. Once it was better, and it would be again. If I could just stop being bad. . . .

I didn't bother my parents for a long time after that. I didn't feel too good. My shoulder hurting made me feel sort of sick to my stomach, so I stayed in my room on the bed. Sometimes my mother would look in on me, but Father was always calling her to get him something.

*Don't baby the boy. Leave him alone.*

It hits me.

My parents didn't send me here. They don't know where I am. They must be so worried because even though they don't see me while I'm in the basement, they know I'm there, all right. Especially Mother. But now I'm not there, and they don't know where I am. I have to find them.

I'm not supposed to be here. That was a mistake. My mistake—because I went outside. Because I let the door slam and couldn't get back in. My mistake. I'm always messing up.

Father warned me about going outside. He never let me go there. I knew the reason, he said. *Danger*.

I tried to listen, tried to do what he said.

But outside was where the birds were. It was where you could walk forever. The air was fresh, and a gust of it could make you want to run. *Danger* was a meaningless word—an interesting sound. I went outside whenever I could until—

The first chance I get, I'm getting out of here. I'll find our house, figure out a way to get back in the basement. My parents will be so glad to have me back, they'll let me live upstairs again. They'll make the spider stay in the basement. And I won't ever go outside again. I promise.

Dr. Leidy comes back to her seat. She smiles at me.

"Does your shoulder hurt?" she asks.

The spider moves. I don't answer.

"The doctor wants to have it X-rayed when you're feeling a little better," she says.

Whatever that means. "Do you remember hurting it?"

"It's fine," I say. But my head isn't.

Dr. Leidy nods her head and writes something on her pad.

"Lunch is coming," she tells me. "The doctor says you can eat." She looks up at the coatrack thing. "You won't be needing the IV much longer."

Lunch? I haven't had lunch since—well, I can't eat it. What if Father found out? An apple here or there from Mother, OK. Even that was risky. But a whole lunch—when other people know? Beyond risk.

"Charlie," says Dr. Leidy, "we haven't heard from anybody trying to find you."

I shrug with my good shoulder. My parents can't do that. It would call attention. *Danger*.

"Why do you think that is, Charlie?"

I shrug again. "Father doesn't like fusses."

"Fusses." Dr. Leidy's voice is matter-of-fact.

I only repeat what I said. "Father doesn't like fusses."

Or messes, I could add. If I wasn't so clumsy. . . . That was the main problem before the basement. I spilled things. And I asked questions. If it had been only that, it wouldn't have been so bad—maybe only a night or two in the basement. I'd been through that.

But I sneaked outside. Outside with the blue-and-white skies, the birds, and the air moving, pulling on my hair. It was so wonderful that day with the air just getting warm, with the earth smelling of mud and new leaves growing. I wanted to stay outside forever. When Father appeared on the back porch, I was on the grass, jumping and laughing. I stopped right quick.

*Get back in here. I told you—*

*But Father—*

*Do you think we need the neighbors asking questions?* Smack! *None of their business who lives here.* Smack! *Now, sit over there until I tell you otherwise.*

I bite my lip. Sometimes it was awful hard to be good enough. I was bad to sneak outside. I knew that before I did it, so I was bad two ways. I know the reason, but I still don't understand it.

"Charlie."

Oh. Dr. Leidy's still here with those quiet, steady eyes. Not worried-looking like Mother. Not like Mother. Quiet, steady eyes.

"Do you want to leave the hospital?"

I nod.

"Then see if you can stay with me here. Tell me why the police found you in the street."

I look at Dr. Leidy. "I don't know why," I say. "I got outside, and—and I lost the basement house. I don't know where it is now."

"You lost your house?" Her steady eyes have narrowed. Doesn't she believe me?

"Yes."

"We'll find it," she says, nodding. "We'll find it for you all right. Can you describe it?"

"Well, um, there's a kitchen and a back porch and a basement and, and um—" What else? "There's pine trees—never mind the pine trees. But there's a um—well, there's a basement. There's more, but I can't think of anything else. The basement had a—" I stop. I'm not mentioning the spider. "There's a basement."

"OK, Charlie," she says. "You're not feeling too good; I can tell that. I have one more question. What are your parents' names?"

That's an easy one. "Robert and Trish."

"Thanks, Charlie. That'll help. We'll talk again when you're feeling a little better."

"My head hurts."

"I know." She shakes her head. "I'm going to stop bothering you now so you can rest."

Good. I feel real tired. I push the heel of my hand onto the pounding place again.

Dr. Leidy stands up. But then I think of something.

"I can draw pictures," I say. "Pictures of Mother and Father. Then you'd know who they are."

"Great, Charlie. I'll give you some paper, and I'll come back after you've had a chance to make your pictures, okay?" She hands me a pad with a pen. "But rest up, first, Charlie," she says. "That's the most important thing." Then—*Clip-clunk! Clip-clunk!*—she starts back for the hall.

But the spider— "Oh!" With Dr. Leidy's back turned, the spider moves her head so that her eyes are full on mine. "Oh, oh!" I don't mean to say it, but her eyes hurt my head and stomach so much. "Oh, oh, oh!" The spider, the spider!

Dr. Leidy turns abruptly. "What's wrong, Charlie?"

I point to the spider. "The spider. Can you make her go away? Please? She's going to get me."

Dr. Leidy walks back into the room. "A spider?" she asks. "Where?"

I point again. "Don't you see her? Big and red and all over the corner? She's looking at me and looking at me." I shiver all over with those eyes on me. I shouldn't have talked about the spider. She doesn't like it, and her red gets darker the more she doesn't like it. "She won't stop looking at me."

Dr. Leidy stares at the spot, then at me.

"She's big?" Dr. Leidy asks.

"Real big. And she wants to kill me. Ohh . . . can't you do something?"

Dr. Leidy comes back to sit next to me. She takes one of my hands in both of hers, all cool over my hot one. "Charlie," she says. "You're having a hallucination. That's something our minds can make up when our bodies are sick. Your mind is making up the spider because of your fever, I bet."

"You don't see the spider?" That can't be true.

Dr. Leidy shakes her head. "No. She's not real."

She is, too. That's what I want to say, but I don't. It's too hard over the pounding, and Dr. Leidy says she can't see her. But she's there. How come Dr. Leidy can't see her? Is this some kind of test, too?

Dr. Leidy looks down at me with those calm, steady eyes. I like how calm and steady they are. I feel like I could say anything, and those eyes would stay calm and steady.

"But," she goes on, "she feels real to you."

Real, real, real.

"Picture this, Charlie." She lets go of my hand and makes a sweeping motion with her arms. "There's a piece of glass I'm putting here between you and the spider. It goes from wall to wall and floor to ceiling. Can you imagine that?"

I nod, looking at where it is.

"You can't see the glass because it's so clean and clear, but it's there, and the spider is stuck on the other side of it."

I nod again, trying to put little shiny places on the glass to make it more true. The spider can't get through. Nothing can.

"Do you feel better?" she asks.

"Yes. Some. Still scared, but not as much."

"You concentrate on that glass," says Dr. Leidy. "Make it as thick and as strong as it needs to be to keep the spider away. That'll help. If you need more help, push that button to call the nurse." She shows me where to push on something attached to the bed. "You'll be fine."

Dr. Leidy leaves then, with me concentrating hard on the glass. And a finger on the button.

# CHAPTER SIX

I coast out of sleep. Food. I smell food. Food?

I open my eyes and push up to see the tray on a table next to the bed. Wow!—a sandwich, some coleslaw, two pear halves, and a small carton of something. Why is this food here? Is this a trick? I'm not supposed to get food like this. Not since the basement.

Well, it doesn't matter. I won't eat it.

I pick up the pad and pen I'm half lying on, shoved into the creases of the blanket, remembering the pictures I need to make. They're important, and I need to do them as fast as I can. Forget this food.

First I draw Mother, parting her soft hair to the side. I give her eyes that half-slanted look, her mouth the almost-smile she makes right before she laughs. It's been a long time since I heard her laugh. When I'm finished, I stare at it. Mother . . . I wish she was here.

I pull the picture off the pad and start Father's, but for some reason, I can't do it.

My head hurts. So does my stomach. And there's the spider, watching, always watching. I drop the pen and stare at the glass Dr. Leidy put up against the spider. The glass gets thicker and stronger as I stare at it.

"Charlie?"

I open my eyes. A lady is here. I must have been sleeping.

"Hiya, Charlie," she says. "My name's Jackie. I'm your nurse today." She takes my wrist in her hand and checks her watch. Then it's my temperature. "Aren't you hungry?"

The food is still here. I turn on my side again and close my eyes. Better not to see it.

"Come on, Charlie," says Jackie. "You have to eat so you can get well."

Jackie pushes a button that raises the bed under the top half of my body. I don't want to sit up. She positions the table the tray is on so the food is suspended over my legs. I watch while she pours milk from the carton into a paper cup. Milk!

"Eat something," she says.

I look from the food to her. She doesn't understand.

"I'm not allowed," I tell her.

"Who says?" Like she's mad.

Ohh! I shudder. The spider's looking at me and won't stop. She's growling deep in her throat—*Ihmm! Ihmm!*—and standing upright. Her free feet move up and down, up and down. They don't move together, but it's like they have different brains. Her growl gets louder, and her feet get bigger and closer until—

"No!" I shut my eyes, but the spider's feet won't go away. They're burning my head, my eyelids, my cheeks. The growl is a roar as loud as the sky, and I can feel the spider's burning breath on my face. I can't get away. I push my back hard against the mattress and turn my head every way, but I'm caught. Trapped!

Jackie—she's my only chance. Can I risk it? Will she help?

Or will she say I brought it on myself and let the spider have me? But that's what's happening—

*IHMMM!*

"The spider!" I yell against the roar. Can Jackie hear me? "Make her go away!"

"Charlie!" Jackie's voice cuts through like a light after a bad dream.

At once the spider's feet leave my face. The roar stops. *Click.* Gone.

I open my eyes. Jackie's face—it looks—I don't know what it means. Her eyebrows are high.

I see the spider. Back in her corner. Waiting again. What happened to the glass between us? Part of it is missing, fading into nothing before it reaches the floor.

"Are you OK, Charlie?"

I'm sweating and my hands shake up to my elbows on top of the blanket. I need to build the glass again, but it's hard when my hands are shaking.

"My head hurts."

"Have your sandwich," says Jackie. "That will help."

I can tell Jackie doesn't see the spider. I see her. See her and feel her. Why can't everybody see her?

I look at the food. Jackie wants me to eat it.

But I'm not allowed. I feel Father's belt across my back. *I told you not to touch. That's not for you!*

"Charlie," says Jackie, "you are allowed to eat. You are."

"That's what you say," I answer, keeping an eye on the spider, "but I'm still not allowed."

"Who says?"

That's what she asked before. Is that what made the spider come over? I check. Those feet are going and going, kneading the air. I concentrate on building the wall of glass again, making it thick and strong so she stays on her side, but I know she will be back. She's only waiting for the right time.

"Do you like being sick?"

"No."

"Then eat. You'll be surprised how fast you feel better with good food in your belly."

"But—" I feel confused. Jackie says I have to eat to get better, but Father—

Jackie takes the sandwich and holds it under my nose. It smells so good. Huh-huh-huh—quick, scared breaths. The bread and the cheese. Oh, the sweetness of it. I haven't eaten cheese since I was sent to the basement. No. One time there was cheese. That was before the lock on the refrigerator. Then only peanut butter. Bread. Water.

Cool water. Rain.

Once, I stood in the rain. I was in the backyard right after the sun went down, so it was dark. No one could see me. I made sure of that. It started to rain—wet and cool, not cold. Little taps at first. I knew I should run inside. I knew the rain was making it worse. But I stayed out there and soaked up the wet, same as the trees and grass, going from dry to watered. I leaned back with my arms stretched wide. The light rain blew into something bigger. I turned and turned into the wet wind, laughing silently harder and harder. This was exciting. This was real. The rain said my name. *Charlie, Charlie, Charlie.* And I answered in joy. I knew what I wanted more than anything was to know the outside, the *dangerous* outside. Because in this wetness was joy and peace.

"Charlie, come back."

Oh, Jackie—and I lose the rain.

Rain. Water.

"I'm thirsty," I say.

Jackie hands me a cup from the tray. I drink it straight down.

"But it's milk." I hand back the cup.

Oh, no. What's going to happen?

"I won't tell," says Jackie. "The wrong person asks, I'll say I drank it. Here." She hands me the sandwich again. "And I'll say I ate the sandwich, too."

*Oh*—huh-huh—two quick inhales. If I could.

"Go ahead," says Jackie. "You already drank the milk. How can eating a sandwich make you more in trouble?"

I don't even want to think about it. But it sure could.

I want the sandwich. I really do. "You sure you won't tell?" I breathe in deep. Maybe my parents won't find out. Anyway, I have to eat something. They don't want me to starve, do they? Otherwise I couldn't have had peanut butter or bread. Maybe not even water. But this food is too good for me.

I check the spider behind the glass.

"Eat. Come on. I have to check on my other patients."

I take a deep breath. Then I grab the sandwich. Gone in three bites. I hardly get to taste it, but it's gone. And it feels so good in my stomach.

A footstep outside the door. Father?

I squeeze my eyes shut and wait. I ate the sandwich. I shouldn't have done that. Now I'm going to get it.

*Don't you ever learn?*

Here it comes.

After a few seconds, I open my eyes again. No Father. Only Jackie. The footsteps move on from the door.

"Good job." Jackie's smiling. Her eyebrows are down, her forehead wrinkles flat and almost gone.

I smile, too. Jackie leaves while I'm still smiling. I check the spider. Still there behind the glass, but the feet are quiet. That's better.

I keep eating while I study the picture of Mother and the one I started of Father. How I wish Mother and Father were really here! Everything would be better. They'd take me straight home, all smiles. *Home.* What a wonderful word.

I pick up the pen and work on Father's picture. I can't get his eyes right, and every mistake means I have to start over. Darn! Try again. Good thing there's lots of paper on this pad.

Wish I had my pencils with their erasers. Wish I had my pencils and the house they're in and the people in the house and the food upstairs and—

I'll go home when Dr. Leidy gets these drawings.

There! Done! There's Father with his dark, straight hair combed back flat against his head. One eye's kind of narrowed like he's thinking hard. Well, he does look like that. Well, not exactly that with that smile I gave him. Too wide, I guess. Oh, well. Close enough.

I put the pictures and the pad on the bed table and think about eating again, but I can't. I'm tired and tired and tired. I check the spider in her corner before dropping onto the pillow. The glass is thinner, but sleepiness softens my fear.

---

When Jackie comes back, I wake up. The light coming in the window is dimmer.

"How are you doing, Charlie?" she asks.

I shrug on my good side.

"I sleep all the time," I say. "I can't stay awake."

"Sleep's good," she answers. "Food and sleep are what you need."

She checks my wrist, my temperature, and she nods.

"I'm going home in a minute," she says. "Someone else will be looking after you."

"Who?"

"It'll be a lady named Sandra."

"Oh." I'm relieved, but why? I don't know Sandra. "Is she nice like you?"

"Even nicer." She laughs a little. "You're a little charmer, aren't you?"

I don't know what that means, but I guess it's good. I laugh with her.

"So eat your food," says Jackie. "Sleep and eat all you want. Ask for more if you're still hungry. That'll be the ticket."

"*Ticket*?"

"That means that's the right way." She starts to leave. "See you in the morning."

She goes, and the room feels empty. Pushing what Jackie calls the IV pole, I get up to use the bathroom that's behind a door in the corner of the room. I sort of remember Jackie helping me get there the last time. I can do it by myself now.

Everything in the bathroom is clean and white except the floor which is green, too. I like green. Dark green like wet grass. But a bathroom. I hope Father doesn't come in while I'm in here. I'm not supposed to use the bathroom. Father never said why. But that was part of the punishment. So if he comes here now, what will I say? But there is no back porch, no pine trees. Not here. And the bathroom door isn't locked against me. So it must be all right. All right enough. Just hope I finish and I get out of here before Father comes, so I don't have to explain.

No Father so far, and I'm back in bed. Tired again. Why is it so much work to walk to the bathroom and back? It's not so far.

I doze off and on, off and on, but don't really get into a hard sleep. Finally I'm just awake. I wish Jackie would come in and talk to me. But she went home.

Lonely here.

Lonely . . .

Someday I will never be lonely. I'll make sure of that. No basements, no hospital rooms. Living upstairs with my parents, eating dinner with them. And when I'm grown up, I'll jog like Father does. Go outside. Jog in the rain. Three, five times a day. All day. Just to feel that wide, forever openness. No walls at all. Maybe I'll live outside. When I'm grown up.

Outside . . . that's what got me into trouble.

I push the pictures of Mother and Father to the side and pick up the pad of paper. I'll draw a picture of Jackie. But halfway through, my arms are tired again. I rest for a while, then draw some more. Rest, draw, rest, draw.

I prop my new picture up between the water pitcher and the cup. There. That feels good.

A tall, gray-haired lady comes in with a tray. She says, "Hi, young man," puts the tray on the table, and leaves before I can think of what to say back.

The food is hot. I'm not sure what all of it is, but I eat it. The green beans are bitter, but I eat every one. Bitter green beans are good. When I'm almost finished, I see something moving in the corner of the room.

The spider. And there is no glass between her and me anymore. It's completely gone. I concentrate on putting it back, but there's a hole in it. I patch it, but another one appears. How can I make the glass wall solid so the spider can't leave her spot?

Well, I'm not eating any more. Eating'll make her come over. I put down my fork. I feel so tired again. There's something wrong about this food business. I can't figure out what it is.

Something . . . but my head hurts, and I just want to sleep. In and out, in and out of dark sleep. I can't keep track. My tray is gone. The IV bag is full again. Then less full. Sandra comes in a couple of times, I think. Too hard to think about it. I give in, and I'm gone.

# CHAPTER SEVEN

A familiar smell comes through the darkness.

"Father?" I sit up quick.

"It's the doc, Charlie. Good morning." He turns the light on next to the bed. Doc Patel.

"Oh," I mumble. "Aftershave."

"Shaved twenty minutes ago." His voice is cheerful. "You're my first patient of the day."

I wonder where Father is while this man is here. It seems that if there is a man here at all, it ought to be Father. But it's not.

The doc listens to my back and chest like before. I don't like it that he has to touch me. I understand that's the way things are, that he's doing what he's doing to help me, but I don't like it. It makes me nervous, and my teeth start to chatter like I'm cold, but I'm not.

Doc Patel takes the stethoscope away from his ears and lets it hang from his neck. "How are you feeling?" he asks.

"I don't know. Bad."

"Say *ah*." Dr. Patel holds my tongue down with a flat stick and peers down my throat. The stick makes me cough. Then the doc puts some pointy thing with a light in it inside my ears, one at a time, to check them. "Hmm."

I look up at him, and he's frowning.

"Your infection's not responding to the medicine. We'll put you on something else."

I nod. *Infection—medicine—*only sounds in the air. The meanings separate and fly like butterflies away from the words.

I watch the butterflies—gold and orange—fly away so free. I want to chase them in the sunlight and be free, too.

The doc's voice pulls me back, and the butterflies fade. "When we get rid of that infection, your fever will go away."

I nod again. I'm sad that the butterflies are gone.

"Don't you worry, Charlie. Pretty soon you'll be out of the hospital and in a good place, getting ready for the holidays just like everybody else."

"Holidays?"

"Sure. You'll be fine real soon." The doc puts his pen in his shirt pocket and smiles down at me. "Eat your food and think good thoughts."

He winks at me and turns off the light. Now he's gone.

When I open my eyes again, streaks of sunlight brighten the room. I remember all that happened when the doc was here. Why does he start his day in the dark, I wonder. I sit up and stretch. Makes me kind of dizzy, so I lie back again.

Images of Mother and Father shift behind my eyelids. Mother—soft and quiet and worried. Always worried. Father—loud footsteps and firmness. Never changes his mind or even the direction he's walking.

*Don't get in my way!*

But he used to tell jokes, too. Back before we moved. All three of us would laugh.

*What eats shoots and leaves?*

*A panda.*

Even Mother would stop looking worried. I miss his jokes.

Why haven't they found me? If I could be with them, everything would be all right. I know this. The infection would go away, and I could go home again. Live upstairs. Eat meat loaf, baked potatoes, green beans. Feel good. And I would stay inside. No matter what.

I hear the shuffle of feet at the door, and Jackie comes in. She takes the IV tube off the end of the needle. "All through with that," she says. "Good job."

I watch as she changes the tape around the needle.

"Why can't you take out the needle if I'm through with it," I ask, "and not just the tube?"

"That's in case we need to start up another IV in a hurry," she answers. "It's what we do with everyone. There." She pats my arm. "All finished. Someone will be here in a minute with a wheelchair to push you down the hall," she says.

"Why? And what's a wheelchair?"

"A chair with wheels. You'll see it and you'll know."

"But why do I have to go down the hall?"

"This room is for kids who need more attention than you do. Hey." She picks up the picture I drew of her. "This is pretty good. May I have it?"

"Sure," I say. I can draw another.

"You've made my day." Her face looks all soft and pink. "Thanks."

She takes the picture with her, holding it carefully, a smile on her face. I didn't know she would care about that. Just a picture. Anyone could draw one. Right?

So—a wheelchair. That's what I first see coming into the

room, but it's pushed by a tall man with a thick black mustache and almost no hair on his head.

"I'm Larry," he tells me. His voice is so deep I almost can't hear it. But I like it. So warm sounding, it makes me think of the brownies my mother baked at the lake house.

I sit in the wheelchair so Larry can push me to my new room. I take the pad and pictures I drew from the bed table and hold them in my lap. I guess Dr. Leidy will find me down the hall.

"I can walk," I say.

"Sure you can." But Larry pushes me just the same.

I keep turning around to look at him. His teeth take up most of his face when he laughs. I didn't know people could smile so wide.

He's laughing now. "They say push the kid in a wheelchair; I push the kid in a wheelchair."

I laugh, too, but I'm not sure what's funny.

In through a doorway. New room, different window, and two beds. One of them taken. Plus there's a big radio on the wall making noise and flashing pictures.

The boy in the other bed waves as I get pushed by.

"Now, you two make friends," says Larry. He takes the papers and pad from me before settling me in my new bed. "Hey," he says, "nice pictures. The lady's your mom, right?"

"Mother," I correct. "How do you know?"

"You've got those same big eyes." He puts the papers and pad on the bed table and helps me into the bed. "All right, kid. Breakfast'll be here soon." He stands back to look at me. "You OK?"

"Just hot," I say, because I'm sweating again. Why? I hardly did anything. Larry did the work.

Larry pours some water into a cup from a pitcher on the bed table and hands it to me. "You'll feel better in a minute. Getting up and down can wear you out if you're sick." He waits until I drink the water before leaving with the wheelchair.

The other boy reaches for something on his bed, and the noisy box goes dark and quiet. "Hi," he says. "I'm Aaron. Aaron Horowitz."

I look at him. He's got something hard and white around one arm, and cuts and bruises cover half of his face. One eye is almost swollen shut. What did he do wrong?

"I'm Charlie."

I've seen other boys before—watching from the living-room window—always staying back in the shadow. That was the rule.

*If they see you, they can get you!*

And girls, like the bike rider across the street. Her bike was blue, almost as dark as a night sky, and she was a streak going by sometimes. I wondered where she was going. But she moved away. When she left in the car to follow the moving van, I waved. It was one time I was right up at the window. It wouldn't matter, I thought, since they were all leaving, but the girl probably didn't see me, anyway. I missed her and her bike after that.

*Kids! Nosy kids!*

The big kids at the lake house—

"What's your last name?"

Aaron Horowitz again. With that same question.

"Charlie. Just Charlie."

He props himself up on his free elbow.

"Why don't you want to tell me your last name?"

"I don't have one," I say.

"Everyone has one," he answers. "Did you get hit on the head or something?"

"No. Well, once, but that was because—" I don't finish, don't tell him how Father was in a hurry, how I came out of the bathroom at the wrong time, how I hit the light switch with the back of my head. I don't say this. Just think it.

*You can't get in my way. I've told you that. You have to keep a clear path. Now you know why.*

I used toilet paper to stop the bleeding while Father went on down the stairs. I heard Mother's footsteps run halfway up before Father called her back.

*You can't baby him all the time, Trish, or he won't learn. Now, finish getting my coffee. Trish. Get my coffee.*

And her footsteps went slowly down again.

I'd forgotten to listen before opening the bathroom door. I never did after that.

"Charlie?"

Hmm? Oh, yeah. Aaron Horowitz. I look over at him.

"Well, what are you doing here? I got hit by a car." Aaron closes his eyes a second. "I think my mother's still screaming."

"Did she get hit, too?"

He gives me a puzzled look. "No. She had a problem with me bleeding all over the street. Doesn't that make sense?"

A lot of things don't make sense. His mother can scream and make a fuss? Wouldn't his father mind?

"I got sick." That's the easiest thing for me to say. "They keep bringing me food."

Aaron Horowitz curls his lip. "Awful, isn't it?"

Awful that I'm breaking a rule by eating all this food? Or that the food is awful, or awful because I'm sick?

I don't know what's awful, so I don't answer. Right now what's awful is how I feel—hot and sweaty and having to talk to someone. It's so much work. And I don't know Aaron. I shouldn't be talking to him, anyway. He doesn't seem to know that.

"My mom says we're having a Thanksgiving dinner when I get home," he goes on. "Cranberry sauce and everything. Just in time for Halloween."

"I don't know those words."

He sits all the way up. "What words?"

"I don't know. *Cranberry. Thanks*-something. *Hallowie.*"

"Everybody knows what those are."

I don't care. I turn on my side and just sweat. Maybe if I stop talking, things will settle down like Larry said.

# CHAPTER EIGHT

I'm eating a peanut-butter-and-jelly sandwich with Mother and Father at the lake house. From the screen porch, we're watching the pine trees sway in the wind. Father is smiling at Mother and she's smiling at me. I'm smiling at my wagon, my shiny, red wagon which is sitting, with all its four wheels, beside one of the trees. I know without looking that the wagon is half full of leaves and acorns and pinecones. I put them there.

*Clanka-clank-clank!*

Noise from the hall wakes me up, and the lake house is gone. I didn't even know I was sleeping.

A lady brings my breakfast tray through the doorway and onto my table as I sit up. She leaves, and I look over at Aaron. He's already eating, but he waves with his fork.

"Feel better?" he asks.

"Yeah." But real tired. My arm is heavy when I reach for a roll.

"My mother was here while you were sleeping. She said she heard you ran away."

"No."

"Well, why were you wandering around outside in the middle of the night?"

"I wasn't wandering around." I don't explain. It's too hard. "But you were outside, too, weren't you?"

"What, you mean when I was hit by a car? It's hard to get hit by a car indoors."

"Well, then."

Aaron looks puzzled and shakes his head.

I finish the roll and start on the applesauce. I used to eat a lot of applesauce. Cool and sweet and slides right down. I think of the apple hidden behind the cookbooks. Is it still there? I hope I can still find it when I get back to the basement.

"My soccer team played yesterday," says Aaron. "We lost. Two–zip. Wish I'd 'a' been there."

I don't know what any of that means, so I just keep eating. I like eating.

"You play soccer?"

Shake my head.

"You should. It's better than football. Football's all stop and start, but you just go in soccer. You can just *be* soccer."

"Oh."

The cereal's good, but I don't know what it is. Everything tastes good. What's Father going to say when he finds out what I've eaten? *Palm against my cheek.* I cringe. *What did I say?*

"What's the matter? You got a pain?"

"I-I was just thinking of something."

"Must have been pretty bad. You looked like something bit you."

"No. No pain."

I start to eat the banana, but I can't think—Father—

"Can I ask you a question?" asks Aaron.

"Sure." I put the banana down and push away the tray. Shouldn't have eaten what I did.

"Are you in some kind of trouble? My mother heard that you don't even know where you live. You must be in some kind of trouble if you don't know that."

"I don't know what's going on," I say. "I thought this was part of the punishment. I thought my parents would come get me." So I could go back to being locked in the basement until Father says I can come out. I don't say that part out loud. Somehow I don't think Aaron would understand. And it's not his business. That's what Father would say.

"You're not being punished. Is that what you think?"

"Well—I don't know. And there's the spider. Oh, forget it." I didn't mean to mention the spider, but she's always there, and I can't get the glass back in place no matter how hard I think about it. Maybe when Dr. Leidy returns, she can put it back for me.

Aaron goes back to eating, and I go back to not thinking. There's noise from people talking in the hall and something loud beeps. It goes *beep-beep,* wait wait wait, *beep-beep,* wait wait wait—

"Halloween's the day after tomorrow," Aaron says, and the sounds in the hall get quieter. Why is that?

I look across at Aaron. He's frowning.

"What's the matter?" I ask. Doesn't he like it quieter?

"I won't be able to trick-or-treat. My mom won't let me go even if I am home—not with this arm and being banged around the way I was." His voice is low and sad. "My costume's all ready, hanging in my closet. I'll be too big for it next year."

"I'm sorry." I don't know what he's talking about.

"Yeah. But—" He brightens. "My mom's making a Thanksgiving dinner for Halloween. Isn't that funny? Maybe I'll go trick-or-treating on Thanksgiving." He looks at me and grins. "You can come with me."

I'm surprised. Go with him where? But something about Aaron's voice makes me just smile. "Sure," I say. I don't know what I'm saying sure about, but I'm saying it. "Why not?"

And he starts to laugh. "That," he says through his ha-ha's, "is the funniest thing I ever heard—trick-or-treating on Thanksgiving."

And, even though it makes my head hurt, I laugh right along with him.

A tall man, bigger than my father but not as big as Larry, strides into the room. He looks just like Aaron, except he's so big. Curly black hair, ears close to the head. Wide smile.

"Hiya, kid," he says to Aaron.

"Hi, Dad," Aaron answers.

The man, I'm guessing he's Aaron's father, bends over Aaron and gives him a long hug with closed eyes and eyebrows pointing up in the middle. Then he straightens up again, running his fingers through Aaron's already-messy hair.

It makes my chest hurt to see. I don't know why. I try not to look, but I can't help it. I wish Aaron's father would come talk to me. Why do I feel like this?

"Doing better?" he asks.

"I'm good, Dad, really. Ask them if I can go home with you. I can be ready in five minutes."

*Dad* must mean *father*. But it feels different. *Dad. Dad.* But I don't see my father with that word, only Aaron's. And why does Aaron say *I'm good*? Was he bad like me?

"Probably tomorrow." The man's eyebrows flatten. Almost like two straight lines over his eyes now. I'd need a lot of pencil to draw them; they're so thick and dark.

"But nothing hurts except the arm. And my head sometimes. I promise. I'm good."

*Good?* It must mean something else.

"I'm glad. But they want to watch you a little longer. Make sure nothing inside is wrong."

Aaron frowns. "I'm out for the rest of the season. I can't play with this arm."

"I know."

"Darn car." Aaron looks angry. Is he allowed? I watch his father.

"Yeah. Darn car." What? He's angry, too, but not with Aaron. This feels weird.

"And my team lost yesterday. Mom said. I should have been there."

"Listen, Aaron. Things happen. You'll play when you're all healed." Those thick eyebrows go back up, and he runs his fingers through Aaron's hair again. Gentle, not harsh. "I'm just glad it wasn't worse."

My father never ran his fingers through my hair. Did he ever hug me? Mother used to. *Trish! You're babying the boy. Let him go.* But Father? I try to think. He must have. Right? But I can't remember.

"Dad, meet Charlie. This is my dad, Charlie. Mr. Horowitz."

"How're you doing, Charlie? Nice to meet you."

"Thanks."

"Charlie can't remember where he lives," says Aaron. "He was hit on the head or something."

"I don't think so," I say. "I don't remember getting hit on the head." Except that one time. That was so long ago. Besides, I can remember where my house is. I just don't know how to find it.

"Well, I'm sure it will come to you soon. These brain injuries heal." Mr. Horowitz's voice is cheerful.

He sits on the edge of Aaron's bed. They talk about stuff I don't understand—the World Somethings. I stop listening.

But I keep thinking. I like Mr. Horowitz. Only he doesn't act anything like my father. He doesn't yell at Aaron or hit him for causing a fuss, for making him come to the hospital.

I know that's why my father hasn't come. He doesn't like fusses. He doesn't like having things in his way. He doesn't like slowing down. He's fine as long as I don't make him change what he's doing. But isn't this the way all fathers are?

I'm confused.

Maybe Mr. Horowitz doesn't want to cause a fuss in front of me. Maybe if Aaron was alone, he would be yelling at him. Or hitting him. It doesn't feel like it, though.

Mr. Horowitz is here. Where's my father? My mother? And Mr. Horowitz sits right on the bed, next to Aaron, touching him even, like that's all he wants to do, like he can't do it enough.

My hands begin to shake. Something bad is going on, and I—and I can't stand it. The spider is as tall as the ceiling and as wide as the room. What can I do? Where can I go?

I turn my head away from what's evil and bury my eyes in the pillow, waiting and scared. How can I get away?

# CHAPTER NINE

The spider is smaller when I reopen my eyes, and Aaron's father is gone. Aaron has that picture radio on. He turns it off when he sees me looking at him.

"You fell asleep again," he says.

"I keep doing that," I say. "I fall asleep all the time. I wake up, and that's how I know I've been sleeping."

"You probably need all that sleep so you'll get better."

"Yeah. But the fever won't go away."

"It will." He sounds like he knows. How does he know?

I nod like I know, too, even though I don't. "I'm so tired of it."

"You said something about a spider before," says Aaron. "Did you get bitten by one?"

"Not yet." I see her in the corner. I hate seeing her there.

"What do mean *not yet?* Do you have an appointment to get bitten?" He laughs a little with the question, and I smile. I guess it did sound funny to say *not yet.* Not that it really is.

"Dr. Leidy says she's not real. My fever's making her up. But I sure see her, and I think she's real. I think she's going to kill me, made up or not."

"Where is she?"

I look in the spider's direction because maybe pointing's a bad idea. "She's always there. Waiting and watching."

"Let me see."

Aaron's out of his bed and on my side of the room, holding the back of his long shirt closed.

"I hate this pretend piece of clothing," he says. "I don't know why I can't wear my pajamas from home. At least the bottoms."

"Yeah." I used to have pajamas. Those old shorts of Father's were all I had for a long time. I wonder what happened to them. And the towel. Father will want to know. Can't waste anything.

"Where's this spider again?" Aaron asks.

Hoping she doesn't notice, I nod at her in the dark corner. Aaron closes in on the space, examining it up and down.

"Don't get too close," I warn. "She's bad. She'll hurt you."

"No, she won't."

"You don't see her."

"I'd like to see this spider. Something so scary and big."

"You would not. She's been after me this whole time. I keep trying to get away from her, and I can't do it. She wants to kill me."

Aaron sits down on the edge of my bed, the way his father sat on his. "Draw her for me. She sounds like a good Halloween costume."

"What's Halloween?"

"You really don't know, do you?" He hands me the pad from the bed table. I guess it's mine now. "Don't your parents ever let you outside?"

I think of how the last time ended.

*Charlie! Hurry up!*

I ran out of the rain to the kitchen where Mother was waiting. I pulled off my soaked T-shirt and traded it with her for a towel.

"Hurry," she said. "Hurry. Father's right out front. Oh, Charlie, he'll send you to the basement for sure."

I moved as fast as I could, but suddenly—

"Charlie!" Father was there with us, and his voice was a roar. "Look at this *mess!*"

Water and a few stray leaves clung to my feet. "I'll clean it up, Father." I say it fast. "It'll be OK."

But he never answered me. Only opened the door to the basement.

"Robert!"

"He's ruined, Trish. I've told you all along. Ruined. Bad. Charlie, this was your last chance. You were warned about going outside. You used to listen. Back at the lake house. You knew how to listen then. Maybe you'll learn again if you're down there long enough."

And that was it. No more chances. Only the basement for—it felt like forever. . . . So dark down there.

"Charlie?" Aaron's voice.

I shake my head to clear it. I don't want to remember that stuff.

Aaron's looking at me. Oh, yeah. He asked me if my parents ever let me go outside.

"My father says only bad kids go outside." It feels funny to say this out loud. But I was bad. Why'd I have to be so bad? Why couldn't I learn?

"Huh?" Aaron gives me a strange look. "Everybody goes outside. *I* go outside. I'm not bad. How could you play soccer if you didn't go outside?"

"I don't—"

"Hey. Don't you go to school?"

"What's *school*?"

Aaron looks at me almost through his eyebrows, his head is down so low. "You don't know what school is? How old are you, anyway? Ten, eleven, twelve?"

"How old are *you*?" I'm feeling resentful. What does it matter how old I am?

"You don't know how old you are, do you? I'm twelve. Will be in a couple of days, anyway. November first. Day after Halloween."

I don't know what *November first* means, but I don't say. Aaron uses lots of words I don't know.

"What's school?" I ask again.

"School—" Aaron stops to stare at me like he doesn't believe I'm real. "Man, school's school. Everybody goes to school. You have to."

"I don't. I don't even know what school is."

Aaron opens his mouth to answer, but he closes it again. Then he says, "Draw me this spider. Let me see this awesome thing."

I take the pen and touch it to the paper. In the corner of the room, black mixes with the spider's red. Her feet move.

"I don't know if I should. She's getting madder. She'll get me if I show you what she looks like."

"No, she won't. I'm right here, and I won't let her. If you draw her, she won't be so strong."

"How do you know?"

"I just do. Draw her picture."

I hope Aaron's right.

I turn my head so that I can't see the spider. Nothing can keep me from feeling her, though.

I draw her. Big and round with ugly eyes and all those legs, waving and waving. I hear her growling from the corner. *Ihmm!* My heart beats faster.

Aaron stands so he can watch over my shoulder. I wish he wouldn't stand so close, but I hold down the nervousness it makes me feel. "She's got a lot of legs. Real spiders—I mean the ones I've seen—only have eight."

"She's not your normal spider." I draw the bent-finger markings on the spider's back extra dark.

"They look like sevens."

"Sevens." I try out the word in my mouth. I know about seven that you count, but he must mean something else.

Finally, I'm done.

"She's not really black." I tilt the pad so Aaron can see better. "More a dark red. She gets darker when she gets mad."

Aaron tears off the page while I hold the pad. "She's one scary critter," he says. "Reminds me of some nightmares I've had." He looks down at me. "Do you care about this drawing?"

"I hate it."

Then Aaron bites on one end of the paper and pulls on the other with his free hand. He rips the paper in two.

"Hhh—you can't do that." I try to grab it back. "That's just going to make her so mad."

Aaron gives me half. "Look at your spider in the corner. Is she any different?"

Hey. She's a lighter shade. Not so hard around the edges, either.

I rip my piece in half. I rip the halves in half. Then again—faster and faster as the spider fades. Only tiny pieces are left. Aaron gives me the other half, and I rip that up, too. I laugh and laugh, ripping and ripping until there is nothing left to rip.

Aaron picks up a bunch of the scraps from the bed and throws them into the air. "Happy New Year!" The pieces slide sideways into the air, like leaves, falling slower than they went up. I pick up a handful. "Happy New Year!" Picture pieces scatter all over.

And the spider—she has only an outline left. That makes me laugh some more.

Aaron laughs with me until Sandra comes in.

"What's all this noise?" She looks at the tiny pieces of paper all over the floor and on the bed. There are two on Aaron's black hair. Lines form between Sandra's eyebrows. Uh-oh. Now we're going to get it. We should have known better. I should—

Aaron starts to clean up the floor. "Sorry," he says. "It was my idea." He looks at me. "What's the matter? You got another pain?"

I move my head from side to side, but I'm waiting for Sandra to be angry. *Charlie! What have you done? Get over here!* Sandra looks at me and shakes her head.

"Almost time for you guys to go home, I guess." She has the trace of a smile on her lips. "You must be feeling pretty good if you're making messes."

I let out a breath I didn't know I was holding. She's not angry. And we made a mess.

Aaron stands up straight, his free hand full of paper. He grins at me. "Happy New Year!" he cries, and there's paper flying once more. Some of it lands on Sandra's hair.

"OK, Aaron," says Sandra. "Now clean it up for real."

I start to help, but Sandra says, "No, Charlie. You stay still."

"But I feel better," I say.

"Good," she says. "Let's keep it that way."

When Aaron throws the trash away, he spots the pictures of my parents on the bed table. "Did you draw these?" he asks.

"Those are my parents," I say.

He picks up the papers, his good hand kind of propping them up against his bad one. The bad one works, I see; it's just that the arm attached to it can't with that hard white thing on it. "You're really a good artist."

"He sure is," says Sandra. "Now, come on, you two. I have to take your vitals."

I look at her.

"Your temperature," she explains. "Your blood pressure, your pulse."

"Look at the pictures over there," I say, and Aaron wanders back to his bed, looking at my drawings the whole time.

"These are really good," he says, while Sandra takes my vitals. "You make them look like real people." What else? Oranges? Wagons?

"Do you recognize them?" I ask.

"No, but I'm sure somebody will. Things are going to work out for you, Charlie. Your parents will be here before you know it."

I take a pill while Sandra watches. Then she takes Aaron's vitals and leaves the room.

"You really feeling better?" asks Aaron from his bed.

"Yeah. Kind of tired. That was fun, though." I don't say that ripping the paper made the spider almost go away. Saying it out loud could make her come all the way back.

"Good." He lies back on his pillow. "It *was* fun."

Lunch comes, and Aaron explains to me about the picture radio and school and Halloween and Thanksgiving. I can't take it all in. There's so much. Why don't we have a TV in the basement house? And why don't we have Thanksgiving and Halloween? And Happy New Year!? Father probably . . . but I can't think what Father probablies. He must not like all that stuff. But Aaron makes it sound good. Real good.

"I don't understand. You say everybody knows about this stuff?"

"Well, I guess babies don't and people whose parents never let them outside." He glances sideways at me. "You know, it's against the law to keep kids out of school. Of course, if you were homeschooled, that's different."

"How would I know?"

"Can you read?"

"Mother was teaching me for a while, but then Father said to stop." It was after those big kids came to the lake house. "He took away all the books because they would lead me into evil. That's what he said. Reading would turn me into a bad person." Like the big kids. "He said I could try again later when the danger had passed."

"What?" Aaron's eyes almost pop out of his head. "What

danger?" He picks up something from his bed table and holds it up. A thick book with a hard blue cover, not like my old ones. "I read, and I'm not a bad kid."

"Father has some of those big ones," I say. "I've seen them." Aaron's eyes move as he looks at what's inside the cover. "Let me see, too."

He turns the book around. No pictures. Only black marks on white paper. Too far away for me to read, but I can't remember how the letters work anymore. "*Huckleberry Finn*," he says.

"What's that mean?"

"That's the name of the book. The name of the person in it, too." Then he looks back inside the book. *"You don't know about me, without you have read a book by the name of 'The Adventures of Tom Sawyer,' but that ain't no matter."*

"Huh?"

"I'm reading to you. Listen. . . . *The Widow Douglas, she took me for her son, and allowed she would sivilize me; but it was rough living in the house all the time, considering how dismal and regular and decent the widow was in all her ways; and so when I couldn't stand it no longer, I lit out."*

*"Lit out?"*

"That means he ran away," explains Aaron.

*"What?"* No wonder Father wouldn't let me read, getting ideas like that. My father would smack me if—

I feel myself getting all red, and my hands begin to shake.

"What's the matter?" asks Aaron.

"What you read." Father—

"Hey, take it easy, Charlie. It's a made-up story."

"Well, why would someone even make up something like that? You run away, and—"

"And what?"

I stop. "Bad things happen."

"You ran away."

I don't answer. Then I say, "No, I didn't."

"Well, what did happen?"

"Nothing."

"Right." He looks at me across the room through his eyebrows. "You're here because everything's fine."

"Well, it's almost nothing."

"Almost nothing has your picture in the newspaper, did you know that?"

"I'm in the newspaper? That's great! Father reads the newspaper. Maybe he'll see me in it."

"He probably will."

"And he'll come and get me. I'll get to go home."

"Yeah, Charlie. I'm sure that'll happen. But if you didn't run away, how come you're here?"

"I got locked out. I couldn't get back into the house. That's all. People found me outside. I'm sick, and I don't know how to get home."

"You can't call?"

"Call?"

He rolls his eyes. "This—" he picks up a flat, whitish thing on his bed table, "is a phone."

"Telephone?" I pick up something on my bed table that looks like the whitish thing in his hand, only mine's a light green. I hadn't noticed it before.

"Same thing. So you know about phones."

"Well, we have one," I say, "only it looks different." I make a curved shape in the air with my free hand. "Father keeps it locked in a drawer. I've seen it a couple of times. What?"

The corner of Aaron's upper lip rises higher and higher as I speak.

"This is too much for me," he says. "I'm going to read a little, OK?"

"Wait. You said something about calling."

"Sure. Call your parents."

"How?"

"You're holding a phone. Push the number for the one at your house. Then start talking when someone answers."

I slouch back down on my pillow. "Father's doesn't have a number. At least I don't know it if it does."

"Sorry, buddy," says Aaron. "I don't know how else to help you. But your picture's in the paper. Your parents will find you."

Aaron begins reading, and I'm left staring into space. If I only knew the number. How could I? But what if I did? Father would open the drawer and answer. I'd tell him where I am and he'd come here right away. Wouldn't he?

I wish I knew that number. But maybe the newspaper picture will do it. He'll see my picture, and I'll be home soon. Maybe.

Hot again. I push off the covers and drink some water. Now I'm cold, so I put the covers back over me again. I am so sick of the hots and colds.

An infection. That's what the doctor said.

I look at the spider. She's firm around the edges again and dark. At least she's staying in her corner. I want to draw her picture once more so I can rip it up and make her fade. Maybe if I do it enough, she'll disappear for good. I sit up and reach for the pad, but my arms ache. Everything aches. I drop back onto the pillow. I don't have the energy to do anything else.

But the spider . . .

She's not real, Charlie, I tell myself. She's not real.

# CHAPTER TEN

I'm lying on the bed, not really asleep, but not really awake, either, drifting back and forth from one side to the other. My eyes are closed, but I see a small, maroon dot, a maroon pinprick. It's so small I can almost believe it's not there. But it is there, and I stay still to keep it small. If it gets small enough, maybe it will go away.

*Clip-clunk! Clip-clunk!* Here come those red shoes again. I open my eyes to see Dr. Leidy. Good! I've got the pictures to show her. But Aaron's still got them on his side.

"Hi, Charlie," Dr. Leidy says. She takes the chair next to the bed again. "How are you today?"

I shrug off that question. I don't want to think about it. "I drew those pictures for you. Aaron," I call across the way, "can you bring the pictures over?"

Aaron's looking at them again as he crosses the room. When he gets near Dr. Leidy, he says, "Here," and hands them to her so she can see them, too. "Aren't they good?"

"Wow," says Dr. Leidy. "You're quite the artist."

Then Aaron pushes the hair back from my forehead with his good hand. I jump at his touch, but I don't push him away, even though I want to. I don't think he'd understand that I don't like to be touched. "Look," he says to Dr. Leidy. "That's the same crooked hairline as the man in the picture."

It feels funny to have Aaron and Dr. Leidy looking at me so

carefully. I don't like it, and the maroon dot becomes a pencil point. Still small, but bigger.

"That's a widow's peak," says Dr. Leidy. "Lots of people have them."

"Well, it's a pretty big one," says Aaron, "coming so far down into his forehead like that."

"There can't be many people who have it the way Charlie and his father do," says Dr. Leidy. "That's really a distinguishing feature."

Aaron lets go of my hair and steps back. Good. I push my fingers through my hair, try to shake the bad feeling away. "You look like your father, Charlie," he says, while Dr. Leidy continues to glance back and forth from me to the pictures, "except for your eyes."

"You look like your father, too." I point to his curly black hair, and he grabs a section of it to the side.

"Yeah, so does my sister," says Aaron. "We don't look like my mother at all. Freckles and red hair. That's what she has."

"Well, Charlie." Dr. Leidy's still studying the drawings. "These pictures are going to help the police find your parents for sure." She puts the pictures on the bed table and looks at Aaron. "Would you mind going back to your side while I speak with Charlie?"

Aaron shrugs at me, and I watch him return to his bed. He picks up his book and starts to read.

I look back to Dr. Leidy and see that her eyes are on me. "I have to ask you a couple of hard questions before I send out the pictures," she says quietly.

"What?"

"Do you have any idea why your parents haven't been looking for you?"

I sigh. I'm bad. That's the answer. But if I tell Dr. Leidy I'm bad, what will happen? Will she decide not to find my parents? Will she stop helping me? Will I never see my parents again? The maroon dot grows to the size of a fingertip. Maybe we'll finish talking soon and I can lie still again, concentrating on getting that dot smaller and smaller. That's what I have to do to get it smaller. Be still, quiet, invisible.

"Charlie?"

My parents aren't finding me. I'm by myself. Aaron's going to his house when he's well enough. Where will I go when I'm well? A safe place, Dr. Leidy says, but does that mean home? She doesn't say that. Why doesn't she just say I'll go home? *We'll find your parents, and you'll go home.* Why doesn't she say that? A safe place. Can't that be home? Can't home be a safe place?

"Charlie, what's the deal here?" Dr. Leidy asks.

I don't want to answer, but I don't know what else to do. "I'm bad. I'm being punished for being bad." What's the difference if she knows? Either way, I'm alone.

"No, you're not," says Aaron from his side of the room. "I told you that before. Oh. Sorry." He turns away with a show of reading his book, but I know he can hear everything Dr. Leidy and I say. I don't care.

Dr. Leidy studies me before saying anything. "Why do you say you're being punished? Who's punishing you?"

"Father is. And he won't let me out until the punishment is over."

"Out of the hospital? I promise you, Charlie, your father has nothing to do with who's allowed to leave the hospital."

"I don't mean the hospital," I say. "I just mean—" But I stop. How can I explain this. And *It's none of their business!* That's Father's voice, and it makes the maroon dot darker. *If they see you, they can get you!*

Who? The big kids? Dr. Leidy? Who?

Aaron appears again next to Dr. Leidy. "He was locked in the basement," he says to her. "That's what he's having trouble telling you."

"Locked in the basement?"

"I'd have trouble, too, Charlie," Aaron adds, his eyes looking straight into mine, "if it was me it happened to."

"Stop!" I'm shouting. "I didn't tell you that. How do you know?"

"You did tell me. You said you wanted to get back into the basement for your punishment. You just don't remember, or maybe you didn't mean to say it. It was one of your bad times. I just figured you were making it up same as not knowing about how telephones work and school and stuff. But I believe you now. You're no liar."

"Can you tell me about this, Charlie?" Dr. Leidy's voice is calm. How can she be so calm when everything is so awful? "What happened in the basement?"

"I can't tell you," I say. "Father would be angry."

But I can't help it. So much is pushing against the inside of my head, it all pours out like the water from a gigantic, knocked-over pitcher. And the more I tell, the bigger the maroon dot grows. Bigger and bigger and closer and closer until the spider's red darkness fills the room and there isn't any space left for me at all. I close my burning eyes. I don't know when I stop talking, but I know I do, even though the words go on and on, filling the inside of my head with red darkness.

"He's really sick again." Aaron's voice has a wobble to it that jumps with my heartbeat, and then I don't hear either of them.

---

The light from the window throws shadows across the sheets' creases, mixing and changing darknesses while the spider's low growl moves in and out of the folds like my mother's sewing needle. *Ihmm!-ihmm!*

"Is he all right?" Aaron's voice comes from a long way away.

Jackie's wiping down my chest with a cool cloth, then my face and neck. "He will be," she says, and that makes me feel better. The spider hasn't won, yet.

"Thirsty," I whisper. "Hot."

"I know. Drink some water." She takes away the towel and hands me a full cup. I drink it all. She gives me another, and I drink it straight down, too. "All this is too much for a sick boy to handle," she says. "They should be leaving you alone."

The spider's not moving. Just sitting, waiting for another chance, maroon and hot, on the foot of the bed. Nobody sees her but me.

Jackie takes back the cup and returns it to the bedside table.

I reach out and grab her arm. "Don't leave. Don't let her get me."

"I sure won't."

With Jackie guarding me, I turn on my side, keep my knees close to my chest so my feet are out of the spider's reach.

I don't know if I sleep, but I dream of the basement. I'm there, and upstairs is happiness.

# CHAPTER ELEVEN

Dr. Leidy's in the doorway, but I didn't hear her shoes first. I look at her feet. White shoes. Silent shoes. She stands next to me and regards me with those steady, gray eyes. Except they aren't steady. They wobble. Her whole face wobbles. I want to ask her why she's wobbling, but there's a reason why I can't. I forget the reason, but I know it's important. I just get quiet, as quiet as I can.

"Charlie," she says. "We think we found your parents."

I sit up slowly. "You found them? That means I can go home. Everything will be fine." It's hard to talk, but I say one more thing. "You told them where I am, didn't you?"

"They'll be here soon," she says. "Is that all right with you? The police will be here, too, and you'll be safe."

All right with me? Why does she ask me? It can't be my choice. What does she mean—*safe*?

"Charlie? We can tell them not to come in today if that's what you want."

Of course I want to see them. Why does Dr. Leidy think I might not want to see them?

"Let them come," I say with my eyes closed so I can't see the wobbles on her face. "Please let them come." But why do things wobble inside my eyelids?

Voices in the hallway.

"I told you. My wife and I—"

*Father!* Here? I open my eyes and sit up.

"Our son wouldn't be here. He ran away."

Then they're in the room—Mother and Father. Other people come in, too, but I only look at Father and Mother. "Know these people, Charlie?" Dr. Leidy asks.

Father stops dead when he sees me. Mother is with him, wearing her winter coat. She looks so thin, it must be a struggle not to fall down under the weight of her coat. She looks cold and scared and awfully white. Her chin is swollen, and she wobbles. They all wobble, just like Dr. Leidy. Why are they doing that?

Ohhh . . . not real.

My fever, I say to myself, like I'm two Charlies—the talker and the listener. People don't wobble. These people aren't even here. Just like the spider. I'm disappointed. I want them to be real.

I lie back again and watch. I'm curious to see what my mind is making up.

Mother stares at me through the wobbling. She shakes and shakes her head. She's warning me. What's she warning me about? The spider?

"It's all right," I tell her. "The spider's not real."

Did I say that or not? It seems like I did.

I feel Aaron's eyes on me, but I can't take time to look at him. He's probably wondering what I'm seeing, staring where there's a blank wall and a closet. But if I look at him, my parents might not be there when I look back. I want to see them, even if they are wobbly and made up.

"Charlie," says the father thing. "It *is* you. You're so sick."

"Charlie," says the mother thing. "Oh, Charlie." The two of them stare at me from the foot of the bed. "Oh, Charlie," the mother thing says again.

I want them to come closer, but Dr. Leidy is in their way on one side and somebody else is on the other. It's a big man all dressed in blue—a policeman.

The spider starts out of her corner. I'm not afraid of her this time. I know I should be, but I feel not here, sort of. Like I'm outside of this, watching someone else's life. Outside of the wobbly waves.

Then I see. The spider's not coming toward me. Moving slowly—so slowly—one inch at a time to the foot of my bed where the father thing is staring and the mother thing is shaking her wobbly head. Why is the spider going there?

Evil. Evil, dark and heavy, fills the room.

"Charlie," says Dr. Leidy's voice, "do you know these people?"

Everyone wobbles so much. The father thing's face gets skinny, then fat, skinny, then fat. His gaze on me is hard through the rippling air, and he's not smiling. Why should he be? Something bad is going on. Evil. It's the evil that makes everything wobble.

The mother thing keeps shaking her head. Her swollen chin is maroon like the spider. Evil. Bad.

At the center of all of this is my stomach hurting, like there's something hard in it. I can barely swallow, my throat is that sore, and my head aches and aches. That's where all the evil is. Starts in my head and branches out to my stomach and throat and everywhere.

*Fills the room,*
*Makes a tomb,*
*Feel the doom*
*In Charlie's room.*

I would laugh, but it doesn't feel funny. Maybe tomorrow it will.

Even if I am awake, this is a nightmare.

I turn on my side and close my eyes. I don't want to see these parent things, anymore. Maybe they'll all be apples next time I look. Like the apple behind the cookbooks.

Even if the fever did make them up, I wish my parents would at least smile. Act like they were glad to see me. Act happy.

"Charlie?" Dr. Leidy's voice blankets my thoughts. I open my eyes. The people things are still here. I paint smiles on the mother and father things, but they frown through them. Shouldn't I be able to make them smile if I'm making them up?

The spider moves, one scary bit at a time, never stopping, never slowing, closing the distance.

"Charlie, don't you know us?" says the father thing. "We thought you ran away. Why didn't you tell us you were sick?"

The mother thing opens her mouth. Her face gets fat and thin, too. I wonder how she can be so skinny and so fat at the same time.

"Charlie. I'm so sorry." Her voice is rough, like mine when I lived in the basement.

The spider is almost to the line of people things. I want to see what she's doing, moving slowly, slowly like that. They should be afraid. Even if they're not real, they should be afraid.

"I lost you," I say. "I lost the house with you in it." I think I say that.

Then it happens. The spider comes up behind the father thing. All her legs come around him in a hug, and he's *gone!* Gone! I'm so scared my teeth are chattering.

All that's left is the father thing's outline wobbling through the spider's round, maroon body.

I look over at Aaron. He's wobbling, too.

"Stop that," I say. The words hardly come out over the shaking in my voice and my chattering teeth.

"Huh?" His eyes widen, and I look back at the people things.

I know this is my fever making the whole thing up, but I hate it, anyway. Hate it, hate it, hate it. Everything's evil. Maroon and evil.

*POP!* The dark maroon explodes in a bright flash, and the spider is gone. The spider's gone—except she's here. I feel her. She's—

Wait a minute. Father's not the spider. Why did I think that?

I look at Aaron again. He's still wobbling, but he's not made up. He's in the next bed where he's been all along, right there with that cast and bruised face and surprised eyes. He's real. Then—

OH!!!

THOSE ARE MY *PARENTS!*

I move onto my knees through the wobbly air.

"Father," I say. "Mother." I inch forward, trying to keep my balance, across the bed. "You came."

Tears are running down my face. I feel so hot. But this is *real*.

"Take me home," I say. "I didn't mean to leave. I'm sorry I was bad. Please. I'll be good. Take me home."

I reach out my hands. I want to touch Mother and Father. I want them to touch me. They don't move.

"I'll do anything," I say. "Please take me home. Please!"

I feel those invisible but uncuttable lines that have always been between us. Between Mother and Father and me. Because these are my parents, and they love me. I know they love me. They want me back.

I reach my hands to Mother's arms, touch Mother's arms through her coat. Mother's head is shaking, and she's blinking away tears.

"Mother."

She's leaning toward me. What's she going to do?

"He's sick, Trish," warns Father. "Don't touch him. You'll get sick, too."

"Mother," I say again.

Leaning more. One hand lets go of her purse and reaches out.

"*Patricia!*"

Oh, I'm so scared. Father's angry. What will he do? What will he do?

But Mother acts like she doesn't hear. She throws down her purse, and the next thing I know, she's hugging me over the foot of the bed, crying and hugging and sobbing all at once, like she'll never let me go.

I close my eyes against my mother's heartbeat. It doesn't matter what happens now, as long as I have this. What else counts?

"Charlie," Mother says, "Charlie, Charlie, Charlie."

But then the policeman says, "OK, Mr. and Mrs. Porter. That's all." And Mother releases me with a kiss. By the way everyone walks out after that, I know I don't have my parents again after all.

# CHAPTER TWELVE

Somebody yanked the floor out from under my feet. I'm falling and falling with nowhere to land, falling through cold, open air.

Aaron's "Man, man," lines out to me through all that space and steadies the room. I glance across at him. Just the two of us in the room now.

"What happened here?" I ask.

"I don't know." Aaron's shaking his head. "I think your parents are crazy."

"I'm never going home again, am I?"

"Well," he says. "I doubt it. Not where you came from, anyway. Someplace better, I'm sure." He rubs his ear. "You could live with your grandparents, maybe, or an aunt, if you have one. Your mother will get to visit. Maybe. Sometime. I don't know." He's frowning, and his eyebrows point up like his father's did when I first saw him.

"Me, neither." I picture the basement, only now the door at the top of the stairs is in total darkness. No. It just isn't there, anymore. Nothing is there.

The punishment is over, but not the way it was supposed to be. I was supposed to get my parents back. That's what I was supposed to get once I showed I could be good. Now all the basement is, is a cold, dusty place. What could be the point of it now, with no door at the top of the stairs? No one there to tell me—to tell me anything.

"But your fever's coming down." Aaron's voice is brighter.

"Yeah."

"And you're going to be all right. No more basement stuff for you. You're good."

He means I'm fine, but I like it the way he says it.

"Yeah. I'm good." The promise of the basement was everything. I folded myself within its crumbling walls because upstairs was love. Wasn't that true?

"And if you go to my school, I'll introduce you to all my friends." Aaron's voice is higher and faster. Those eyebrows are pointing almost straight up, too. "You can join the soccer team."

"Yeah. Thanks." I wonder where love really is. Good feelings. Happiness. They're someplace, I know. I feel that. But without Father and Mother, how do I get there?

"And you can go trick-or-treating with me on Thanksgiving."

"Yeah." I make myself grin across the room at Aaron. It actually feels good to grin at him. Real good. I grin a little wider and wonder at the grin and at the good feeling that comes from way inside.

He grins back. "That's better," he says.

"Yeah."

I'm good.

# PART TWO

# CHAPTER THIRTEEN

I'm standing at a window in the room they call the solarium. Aaron's been gone a few days, and there's nothing to do.

They say I'm going home soon, too, only it won't really be going home. It will mean living in a different house with a lady named Mrs. Harrigan.

Mrs. Harrigan's all right, I guess. She came to see me, and she smiles all the time. But living in her house makes no sense at all. How can I belong there? I don't know her. Everything's all scrambled.

Dr. Leidy tells me Father and Mother won't be around. I won't be seeing them, and they can't tell me what to do. But I know what to do. Or I did.

I'm confused. My home is a place I've never seen with people in it I don't know. That can't be home.

For me, home means Mother with her quiet voice working in the dining room and Father with that one slanty eyebrow working in the kitchen. Me, working at the kitchen table on my pictures. That's home.

I love drawing. Drawing is the wonderful thing I can do that makes me forget how quiet everything always is. No one gets mad at me for what I say in my pictures, and my pictures get LOUD!

Once I drew some pictures of a squirrel. It wasn't really a squirrel because no squirrel ever looked like that. The squirrel was as big as the tree next to him, and he had the biggest teeth in the world. They were scary, pointed teeth, with sharp ends. The squirrel screamed through those teeth. He jumped so hard the earth shook. It took me a long time to make the ground look like it was shaking, with the leaves and twigs thrown into the air. The squirrel screamed and jumped before biting the trunk of the tree and breaking it right in two. He swung that tree with his paws, knocking over all the other trees with it until he came to a house. Then he smashed that house right to the ground. Smashed it and smashed it until you couldn't tell it had ever been there.

I don't know why I drew those squirrel pictures, but I seemed to need to. I kept looking up to make sure Father wouldn't catch me at what I was doing. I was pretty sure he wouldn't really look, but you could never tell with Father. If he had looked, he wouldn't have liked the pictures; that's for sure.

Once Father came right up next to me on his way through the kitchen when I was working on the drawing of the smashed house. I looked up at him, afraid in my stomach. Was something bad about to happen? What would he do?

Father glanced down at the table, but I could tell he wasn't seeing what my picture was. Not really. His face didn't change, and he just kept going. So I was right. He didn't see. How loud my pictures were didn't matter. What mattered to him was that *I* was still. What he didn't know was that I was anything but still inside my head.

The noise inside my head and body had to go somewhere. That's why my pictures got so LOUD. If the squirrel hadn't knocked down that house, I would have had to do it myself.

Then what would have happened? I can't stand to think of that, but

BASEMENT—

The big room with its musty smells crowds around me until I push it back—back.

I'm not in the basement. I'm in the hospital. King's Hospital. No basement for me. I'm safe. That's what people keep telling me. This is not the basement. Not.

But that's where I would have been if I'd been loud like the squirrel. I would have hurt all over—no, don't think of it, Charlie. Don't think of it.

I hid those drawings under my bed just in case. And I made other loud drawings—gigantic birds with slashing feet, raindrops so big they knocked down trees and houses and men, men with slicked-back hair and one slanty eyebrow.

I didn't smash that house—only in my drawings, but I might as well have. I have no house, no home. No Mother, no Father.

I didn't mean for this to happen.

I want my house back. I don't want to go somewhere else. That house with the basement—that's the place I belong. Not Mrs. Harrigan's house. I want to return to the basement so I can have my chances back.

Does Mrs. Harrigan's house have pine trees in the backyard?

"Charlie?"

I look away from the window. I'd forgotten I was looking out the window because I wasn't really seeing anything.

Grass and cars and trees. No big squirrels. Should have drawn that squirrel killing the spider.

But the spider might have killed me—no, the squirrel—no, me.

I'm confused. There was no spider. Or squirrel.

"Charlie?"

Oh, yeah. It's a new nurse. Tina.

"Time for your vitals," she says.

I follow her back to my room. No Aaron, and the boy in the other bed is sleeping. It's all he's done since he showed up. That's all he's done, but his red-faced mother sits knitting in the chair next to him all the time. She knits real fast, making metal clicky sounds. I hate looking at her, and I don't think she likes looking at me. She frowns and frowns. Sometimes she wipes her eyes, but she never lifts her head, never says anything.

I climb back onto my bed and wait while Tina takes my vitals. She gives me a pill, too, that's still fighting the infection. I'll be taking that for a while even though I feel better. That's what the doc told me.

Push for the television. An orchestra is getting ready to play. It plays every day, so now I know what an orchestra is. Usually I like the music. It takes me places kind of like my drawings do.

The announcer finishes explaining the piece. "And listen for the pedal tones played by the basses," while the picture shows these big, brown instruments as tall as the people playing them. Must be heavy.

A line of those people plays the long, low sounds together.

*Ihmmmmm*. Long and low and dark like the spider's growl. I don't like it.

I turn off the television, but the sounds of the basses stay with me. Low and scary. I wish I hadn't turned on the television. Why did the basses have to sound like that? Why did those people have to play that long, spider's note?

I try to think of something else—trees and wind and rain—the good things, but that dark, scary sound lies under all of my thoughts. I'm thinking that long, spider's note was there all along, but hearing the basses made me know it. Now it won't leave me alone.

*Ihmmmmm* . . .

CHAPTER **FOURTEEN**

---

I'm all dressed in stiff clothes that I've never seen before. The shirt label itches the back of my neck. The pants are too loose, but a belt holds them tight. Borrowed clothes, not mine.

"What happened to the shorts I wore here?" I ask Dr. Leidy.

"I don't know, Charlie," she answers, "but don't worry. You'll get a new pair."

A new pair? Father would let me have a new pair?

Father's not deciding anymore. They keep telling me that. I don't know how that can be. Fathers decide.

"You ready, Charlie?" Dr. Leidy asks.

I nod and sit in the wheelchair like she says to do, holding on to the teddy bear the nurses gave me. "I can walk," I say. I remember saying that to Larry on that other day. But this time I really can walk.

"Hospital rules." Dr. Leidy pushes me out of the hospital-room door, leaving the sleeping boy and his frowny mother, down a hallway past the nurses and doctors and another boy pushing an IV pole. He waves at me as I go past. I wave back. I don't know what's wrong with him, and I don't know his name.

"Bye, Charlie," says Larry. He's wheeling a piece of equipment into another room. "Good luck."

"Thank you," I say.

Dr. Leidy and I take the elevator down to the first floor. It's the same elevator they took me on when I had those X-rays. I'm not so scared of it this time, but I don't like it much, either. My ears feel funny and I hear the basses hum. *Ihmmmmm . . .*

"Now, remember," Dr. Leidy's saying. "You have a session with me next week."

"I remember."

"Anything you want to talk about, any questions you have—"

While she's talking, she pushes me out of the elevator, across a wide area, and right through the hospital doors.

Wa-O-OW!

OUTSIDE! OUTSIDE! It pushes hard against my skin. *Ihmm-ma-ihmmmmm!*

Sunshine, and everything is—is— A hill bright with grass and trees and people— People and cars and—and—

I can't breathe.

My eyes hurt.

My skin hurts.

I CAN'T BREATHE!

I stumble out of the moving wheelchair and race back into the building.

Safe! I don't know what to do now, but at least I'm inside. Safe! Whew! I flatten my back against a white wall and close my eyes to the basses' spider tone, sucking in air, beautiful air. My knees buckle, and I slide to the floor.

Father! He was out there! I felt him! He's so angry, he'll

hit me and hit me. He'll take me home and put me back in the basement. Oh, oh, oh!

"Charlie."

I open my eyes.

Dr. Leidy's watching me with those steady, gray eyes from a chair a little ways away. She doesn't tell me to get up or move or anything. I stay where I am, wishing the floor would open up and drop me into some dark nothingness. A place where I can't see or feel.

"It looks like something scared you out there," Dr. Leidy says.

I gulp and stare at her, not sure what to say. I stand up straight and point out the door. "The outside." My voice comes out in a raspy whisper. "It's so—so big. Too bright."

"You're afraid?"

"Yes."

Dr. Leidy makes a half frown with her lips, and I can tell she's trying to think how to deal with me. "Charlie, do you trust me?"

I shrug. Ouch! My shoulder—but I push that away. "I— yes."

"It's all right to say no," she says. Her eyes are serious.

I look at the floor. It's covered by a green-and-white-striped carpet. "No." Because I'm not sure I trust anybody. I hope it's really all right to say it.

Pause. The elevator opens, then closes. People walk by, scattering words like dry leaves tossed by a breeze.

"Listen, Charlie," Dr. Leidy says. "Life's going to be tough for a while. Real tough."

I nod.

"But you can't stay here. You have to be brave and go out to Mrs. Harrigan's car. You have to go to her house and start learning new things. You have to try."

I'm still looking at the floor. There's a place where the carpet's worn out, and it's all a greeny gray—how all this feels.

Here's what I want to say. "I don't want to go anywhere. I want to go back upstairs with Jackie and Larry." But I don't. It's too hard. And I know Dr. Leidy won't let me do what I want. Can't let me, is what I'm thinking.

"Do you believe me?"

I think about it. Yes. I don't want to go anywhere. I especially don't want to go outside, but I do believe her. So I say yes.

Dr. Leidy stands up. "Come on, Charlie."

She offers me her hand, and I take it as we move forward together. The hum of the basses grows from nothing to everything between my ears. *IhmmMMM* . . .

"Wait," I say. I know I'm the only one who can hear the spider basses. And I can't really hear them. Well, I can, but it's more like feeling them. Or—both. I'm not sure.

We stop while Dr. Leidy looks down at me and I try to figure out how to say it. "Dr. Leidy, what if Father is outside? What if he sees me?"

"He's not outside."

"But what if he is?"

"Then," says Dr. Leidy, her voice still, her eyes steady, "he will have to deal with me." Her face softens, and she smiles at me. "OK?"

I don't like it, but I say, "OK." What can Dr. Leidy do if Father is angry?

The hum gets bigger and my heart races as we walk to the doors, but I make myself go through them. Right outside, it's all too much, and my legs stop. Dr. Leidy stops with me.

"Wait," I say again.

Dr. Leidy's still holding my hand, but I step behind her, trying to hide. I'm glad she's so big. From where I stand, I look all the way down one side, then all the way down the other. No Father. Nobody looking at me at all except Mrs. Harrigan. She stands out with that orange hair. She waves at us from the open passenger door of her red car. Too red.

*Ihmmmmm . . .*

"Dr. Leidy?"

"Yes?"

I come out from behind and stand beside her. "I don't see Father." But I feel him.

"I don't see him, either."

I take a minute to look again. Still nobody I know but Mrs. Harrigan.

"Dr. Leidy?"

"Yes?"

"Can we run to the car? Can we get there real fast?"

Dr. Leidy lets go of my hand.

"I'll race you," she says. "On your mark, get set—"

"Dr. Leidy?"

"Yes?" She's starting to laugh. "What is it?"

"I don't know what that means."

She stops laughing. "It means let's see which one of us can get there first. Ready?" So I go, but she's still talking. "One, two, three—" I stop because she's still talking, "GO!" and she runs straight into me.

We both end up flat on the sidewalk. I get up first. She gets up slower because she's laughing, and, I think, because she's so tall. I don't know what's funny, really, but something must be because I'm laughing, too, even though I knocked my shoulder. But the basses are quieter.

"Oh, Charlie," she says, "you're so wonderful."

By then, Mrs. Harrigan is there with us. "Are you two all right?" she asks.

Dr. Leidy laughs some more and says, "We're just fine; aren't we, Charlie?"

We're walking toward the car. Mrs. Harrigan and Dr. Leidy are talking and laughing together, but I'm looking around, staying close to Dr. Leidy just in case. It's always when I'm not paying attention that things happen. Father's here. I can feel him.

It seems like he's where I'm not looking. *Ihmmmm* . . . I'm just not seeing him. But Dr. Leidy said . . .

We get to the car. I look inside.

No Father. No tricks or tests as far as I can tell.

But there is a little boy sitting in the shadowy backseat. I almost don't see him. His skin is so dark, he blends in. "Hi," he says. "Why'd you fall down like that?"

I look into the sunlight at Mrs. Harrigan and Dr. Leidy. Dr. Leidy's running to the wheelchair. Why? Oh. I left the teddy bear there. When Dr. Leidy brings it back, I see a curl on her head has come unpinned to fall against an eye, and her white skirt is smudged. But she's still smiling.

"Here you go, Charlie," she says. "You don't want to forget this." She gives the teddy bear to me at the same time she gives me a big smile. "Now you be brave for Mrs. Harrigan."

"I'll try."

Then I'm in the passenger seat with the teddy bear, waving to Dr. Leidy. She waves at me while she's still laughing with that half curl blowing across her face. It seems strange leaving her behind. But she said I'll be seeing her soon so she can help me more. At least I know that.

While Mrs. Harrigan drives away, I'm feeling better. I'm in the car, and only Mrs. Harrigan and the boy in the backseat are in the car with me. I'm not sure where we're going, but I'm pretty sure I'm OK right here, right now. In the car. Hardly any spider basses, and I push away the ones I hear.

"Hey, Charlie," says the boy. "Why'd you fall down?" His voice is bright, like he might laugh anytime.

"Say hello to Ambrose, Charlie," says Mrs. Harrigan. "He's your new brother."

I turn around and look at him. His brown eyes are shaped like upside-down spoons. It must take a long time to blink them each time. No. They blink fast just like mine.

"My brother?"

"I already got three," Ambrose says. "They live with my real mother. One of 'em's nineteen. Twins are seventeen. I'm seven. How old are you?"

"Twelve," I say, because that's what Dr. Leidy told me. "Last April," she added, but I don't know what that means. I don't know what *twelve* means, either, except that it's how old Aaron is, too, and it's a word to count with the clock in the living room of the basement house. I don't feel like twelve. I feel like *Charlie* and skin and blood and teeth and hair. What does seven feel like? A green hat? A good night's sleep? And twelve—what's that? A long-sleeved shirt? A windy day? How can these words mean anything about me?

---

During the ride to Mrs. Harrigan's, Ambrose and Mrs. Harrigan talk to each other. I just sit there, listening to the hum of the motor coat their voices, not thinking of anything. I don't want to think of anything.

Mrs. Harrigan breaks into my not-thinking. "Charlie, are you making it?"

That's what Mother always used to ask. Charlie, are you making it? Mother. Will I ever see her again? At least she hugged me before I lost her. At least I got that. But thinking of her and what she said makes me sad.

I sink lower in my seat. "I'm all right," I answer. Is there any other answer?

"You'll be fine," says Mrs. Harrigan. "I take good care of my boys, don't I, Ambrose?"

"Sure," says Ambrose. "It's never cold at Mrs. H.'s, and sometimes she makes oatmeal."

I turn to look at him. "They gave me oatmeal at the hospital," I say. Lumpy whitish stuff, but good.

"I LOVE oatmeal!" Ambrose shrieks. He arches his back

against his seat and laughs loudly. Just like his voice promised. But the loudness makes me nervous.

"Ambrose," warns Mrs. Harrigan.

"Well, I do," he says. His voice is quieter, and I'm glad. I'm glad also that I can still hear the laughing in it. "And, Charlie, Mrs. H. lets you put on milk and sugar and raisins. Lots of raisins. And you can eat all you want. And the house is warm even in the winter. And blankets. You should see Mrs. H.'s blankets. I piled ten on me once while I watched TV. Boy, was that *hot*!"

We get on a big road with room for lots of cars. Green ones, yellow ones, blue ones, and they're all over the place. How can there be so many cars? We're going real fast, and that makes me scared. I didn't know cars went this fast.

When Mrs. Harrigan looks over at me, I'm slouching in my seat so I can't see how fast everything is going by.

"What's wrong, Charlie?" she asks.

"Nothing," I say. Can't tell her I'm scared. *Ihmm-ma-ihmm.* So many basses.

"We'll be home soon," she says.

*Bazoom! Bazoom!* Things go by the car window so fast. In a little while, Mrs. Harrigan steers the car onto a part of the road that splits off from the rest, and we curl around and around until we stop. We go forward again, but now we go slower. Some children smaller than me are riding bikes, and people are out in their gardens. The people next door used to spend time in theirs. I could sometimes hear them talking through the basement's window well.

We turn, and Mrs. Harrigan takes us even slower. Slow

and slower. She brings the car into a driveway and stops it. Everything is quiet. "Welcome home, Charlie," she says.

"Yeah," says Ambrose. "Welcome home."

I don't get out of the car when the others do. Holding on to the teddy bear, I wait until Mrs. Harrigan opens the front door of the house. Then I charge from the car to the house.

"Whoa, Charlie," says Mrs. Harrigan, when I whip past her at the door, but I'm inside.

I breathe deeply and look around. No Father.

Safe?

# CHAPTER FIFTEEN

A narrow staircase with walking space all around it divides the living room from a hallway with doors. Ambrose, whose head barely comes up to my stomach, circles the stairs on a run, stopping to open one of the doors.

"Here's our room," he says. "See?" Inside is what looks like one bed standing on top of another. "You can have the top bunk if you want it."

"I told you, Ambrose," says Mrs. Harrigan, "Charlie's taking the upstairs bedroom." She lifts a box from a chair. "It's my son's old bedroom, Charlie. You'll like it up there." She walks to the first step and signals me to follow.

"Don't go," warns Ambrose. He stands between me and the staircase. "You'll fall on those steps in the middle of the night. You'll hit your head and break your arm. You will."

"Now, Ambrose," says Mrs. Harrigan, "you know I light those steps at night. And Charlie looks to me like he can handle them."

"They're bad." Ambrose's hands are on his hips. "Share my room, Charlie. That's what you should do. Then you won't fall."

"Charlie will be fine on the steps." Mrs. Harrigan continues up the stairs with the box. "You'll be careful, won't you, Charlie?"

"Sure," I say. I remember falling down the steps at home a

long time ago, but I learned to be careful. *Don't run. Don't make so much noise.* "I'll be careful."

Ambrose is frowning and his hands are still on his hips as he watches me go past. Before very many steps, I hear a strange noise and turn around. He's crying. He bolts for his room and *BANG!* slams the door.

I feel scared and push my back as hard as I can against the wall opposite the railing. What's happening? Ambrose's crying hurts my head, and I feel tears starting in my own eyes.

"He'll be all right," Mrs. Harrigan tells me over her shoulder. "Come on."

Ambrose's sobs make me feel bad, but I do what Mrs. Harrigan says. She doesn't act like anything terrible is happening.

The stairs are uncarpeted wood, and we *clump* as we go up. *Clump, clump, clump!* From a window on the landing I can see a large grassy area across the street. It stops where a big building on the other side of it starts.

"That's where you'll be going to school when you're ready," Mrs. Harrigan says. "Beidler Middle School. My son used to play soccer on that field."

"Field," I repeat so I remember. School? Soccer? "Do you know Aaron Horowitz?" I ask. "He plays soccer. He was in the hospital room with me."

Mrs. Harrigan shakes her head. "I doubt if he lives around here. Most people who land in that hospital live pretty close to it."

She takes the next three steps to an open doorway, and I follow her through it. Against the opposite wall is a bed with a pillow and a green-and-orange-striped quilt. I take a deep breath and look at Mrs. Harrigan. Is this room really for me? But she just smiles back.

A dresser with a green lamp on it lines up against the wall cut into by the doorway. Between the bed and the dresser is a blue carpet. Mrs. Harrigan flicks a switch at the doorway and the lamp goes on. It casts a light on a picture over it of a huge bird sitting on a tree branch. I've never seen a bird like that.

"That's a big bird," I say.

"An owl," Mrs. Harrigan answers. "You can hear them around here at night sometimes."

She drops the box on the carpet next to the bed and sighs. "That was heavy." She wipes her face with a handkerchief. "Whew!"

"What's in it?" I ask.

"Clothes," she answers. "Clothes for you. Take a look-see before you come down. Tell me if I've left anything out."

Clothes for me?

She starts again for the stairs. "Make yourself at home, Charlie. I have to check on Ambrose." She shakes her head. Then she smiles at me again. "I'll call you for lunch."

She leaves, and I hear her *Clump, clump, clump!* down the steps while I sit on the bed and feel the quilt. A real bed. Not a hospital bed, but a real bed in a real bedroom. Like what I used to have. Boy, it feels good.

I sit the teddy bear on the bed next to the wall and open the box. Inside is a scrambling of colors. I pull something out. A blue sweater with green stripes. A T-shirt—three of them—two gray and one orange. Underwear. All new. I stop pulling stuff out and just stare at it all.

I've never seen so many new things at once. I don't look at the rest of it. I refold the sweater and the T-shirts and the underwear and put everything back in the box the way it was, before closing it up again. Something's wrong here. These clothes can't be for me. They can't be for me at all. One thing's for sure. Father wouldn't like this. He would really not like this.

Think of now, I tell myself.

I look around my new bedroom. Bookcases where the bed and bureau aren't, and the bookcases are jammed with books. Can this be all right? Aaron says books are OK. He knows how to read even big, thick books. But is he right? Well, it doesn't matter. I can't read, not anymore. Not really. What can I do with a book? Nothing. Out of curiosity, I start to pull one of the books from the shelf.

*Ihmmmmm!*

I push it back without looking at it. *Ihmm-ihmm!* The books and the clothes and the nice room are making me nervous, and I wonder if Ambrose is right. Maybe I shouldn't sleep up here. Downstairs where other people are might be better. Away from the box and the books.

I'm going to ask Mrs. Harrigan if I can sleep on the first floor.

I leave the scary, bookcase room and start down the stairs. I pause to look out the window on the landing.

That's a school over there? It's so big. Why does it need to be so big? What happens in a school? And what does Mrs. Harrigan mean when she says I'll go there when I'm ready? How do you get ready? It's so far from this house to the school. Look at all that space! All that space *where they can get you!* Oh, oh! I know I can't walk across that. Whatever else I know, I know I can't do that. I made it here. That has to be enough. Brrr.

I continue on down the stairs, but *Bam bam bam!* Someone knocking with Father's hard knock is at the front door. It has to be Father. He's going to catch me with the books and the box of clothes. He'll see me in these clothes that aren't mine. What can I do?

I listen, hardly breathing, the basses humming through my head. *Ihmm-ma-ihmm-ma-ihmm-ma!* The door opens, then closes. Now nothing. Did Father come in?

I'm afraid to go down, and I'm afraid to go up. I sit on the steps above the landing so I can't see down the stairs and Father can't see me if he looks up. My heart races, and my palms sweat.

*Ihmmmmm . . .*

Calm down, Charlie, I say to myself. But Father—and my heart is racing and racing. I'm having trouble breathing. Father's not in charge, Charlie. That's what Dr. Leidy said. Don't worry about Father.

How can I not do that? I sure do worry about Father. How do I know I don't need to worry about him? He decides everything.

*Clump! Clump! Clump! Clump!* I push my back against the next-higher step and hold my knees against my chest. Father's on his way up. Father's on his way. If I go back to my room, he'll find me with the books. He'll find me. He'll—

It's Mrs. Harrigan who finds me.

"Why, Charlie! What's wrong?"

I point down the steps. "Father." I can hardly say it.

"Father? You mean *your* father?"

I nod weakly.

"He's not here." Mrs. Harrigan sits down next to me. Her hair smells like flowers, and for some reason, that softens the basses. *Ihmmmmm . . .* "Why do you think he's here?"

"He knocked real loud at the door and—"

"No, he didn't," interrupts Mrs. Harrigan. "That was the UPS man."

"What?"

"A deliveryman. Actually, it was a woman. Nothing to worry about. She always bangs on the door real hard when she's leaving a package. She must have sore knuckles if she knocks everywhere like that." Mrs. Harrigan shakes her own hand out like her knuckles hurt. "My hand would smart for a week after one of those knocks."

"So Father's not here?" I don't care about all the rest of it. I need to know just this one thing.

Mrs. Harrigan looks down at me. "Listen, Charlie, one person who will never set foot in this house is your father. Not if I have anything to say about it." Her face looks so firm.

But I don't understand how she can know for true.

"Charlie." Mrs. Harrigan lifts my chin so she can see my face. My hair is in my eyes, and she brushes it to the side. "Your father doesn't know where you are. He doesn't know, and if he should happen to find out, he's not allowed to come here. Neither is your mother. The judge spelled all that out for them at the hearing. I mean, he explained that to them."

"But—" Nothing is making sense, and all I can do is shake

my head. Father was in charge. How can anyone tell him what to do? And Mother—

Mrs. Harrigan stands up and pulls me up with her. "Listen, Charlie, this is a lot for you to sort out. Give it time, and you'll do it. Now let's go downstairs. I have some nice split-pea soup on the stove."

"With hot-dog chunks in it?" I remember hot-dog chunks in pea soup. Hot pea soup and crackers at the kitchen table. Back when things were good.

"I can put some in," she says.

And we *clump* down the stairs. *Clump, clump, clump!* It's just the noise the steps make when anybody's on them. Me, Mrs. Harrigan, anybody.

The sound of our footsteps change—*k-ch, k-ch, k-ch* (almost silent) as we walk across the carpeting of the living room and the dining room to the kitchen, where Ambrose is sitting at the kitchen table with a book.

"Look, Charlie." He lifts the book. The cover has a picture on it, but I can't figure out what it is. "*The Cat in the Hat.*"

"OK," I say, not sure what he's talking about.

"Put the book away," says Mrs. Harrigan. "You know the rule about books at the table."

"Aw, Mrs. H." But Ambrose gets up and leaves. Then he's back empty-handed.

Mrs. Harrigan places a bowl of soup in front of Ambrose. Steam rises from the bowl. "It will take a few minutes to add the hot-dog chunks, Charlie, if you still want them."

But the pea soup smells so good right now. "Never mind," I say.

She smiles and ladles out another bowlful for me. Then one for herself, too, and she sits down with us. "Let it cool a minute, boys," she warns.

I wait, but Ambrose starts right in. He puts the spoon into his mouth and shuts his eyes. He turns his head from side to side, smiling, with the spoon handle sticking out, no hands, between his lips.

"Good, Ambrose?" Mrs. Harrigan asks.

"Mmm-hmm," comes the answer. Ambrose opens his eyes and pulls the cleaned spoon out of his mouth. "Ahh, Mrs. H., I love you." He dips his spoon into the liquid again.

"I love you, too, Ambrose." Mrs. Harrigan's spoon is still while she smiles at him. Little lines next to her eyes crease while she smiles. I like that.

"Mrs. Harrigan?" I ask.

"Yes?" She lifts up a steamy mouthful and blows on it, rippling the thick, green soup.

"Why does Ambrose call you Mrs. H.?"

Mrs. Harrigan and Ambrose look at each other before looking at me. "Well," says Mrs. Harrigan. She returns the soup to her bowl. "It's easier to say than *Harrigan*, and *Harrigan* begins with an *H*. So he shortens it to *Mrs. H.*"

"*H*," I repeat.

"Yes. You can call me that, too, if you want."

"What's *H*? I can't remember."

Ambrose puts his spoon down on the table and gazes seriously at me. "You don't know what an *H* is?" he asks.

I put my hands in my lap. "It's a letter, right?"

"You can climb up and down all those steps without being

afraid, but you don't know what an *H* is?" Ambrose's voice is full of awe.

"Right."

"Oh, wow." Ambrose slips out of his chair and disappears into the dining room. Right away, he's back, carrying his book. He points to something on the cover. It looks like the inside part of a window. "That is an *H*. It's the first letter of *hat* and *Harrigan*. Right, Mrs. H.?"

I stare at what he's pointing at, but I don't get it at all. How can that little window thing mean anything? It's just a mark. I wish I could remember.

Mrs. Harrigan gently takes the book from Ambrose and puts it on the empty chair beside her. "I don't think Charlie knows his alphabet, Ambrose," she says. "We'll have to teach it to him."

Ambrose points to his chest with his thumb. "*I'll* teach you it, Charlie," he says. "It's easy as anything. You'll see."

"Thanks, Ambrose," I answer. I start eating my soup. It's almost as good as Mother's.

The alphabet. I'm going to learn the alphabet again. Exciting and scary with the spider's hums just outside the room. Do I dare?

"The soup is really good, Mrs. H.," I say. "Real good."

"Thanks, Mr. P." She winks at me. "*P.* for *Porter*."

I don't get it, but I will.

| | |
|---|---|
| Gloom, gloom– | *Ihmmmmm–* |
| feel the doom– | *ma–* |
| feel the doom– | *ihmm–* |
| in Charlie's room! | *ma!* |

It's dark, and my head pounds with this rhyme as I open my eyes. *Ihmm-ma-ihmm-ma-ihmm-ma!*

I hate the basement. Someday I'm going to get out. Someday I'm going to stand in the sun. Someday I'm going to take off all my clothes and stretch out my arms and feel the sun full on my face and all over.

All, all over.

*Ihmmmmm . . .*

Wait.

I sit up.

This isn't the basement. This is a room in Mrs. H.'s house. Isn't it? But it feels like the basement. So dark.

But I'm on a bed. This isn't the basement. Can't be the basement. No bed there. Just a towel on the cold floor. And spiders. Oh, spiders! *Ihmmmmm!*

Not the basement?

If it's not the basement, there's a light switch right over there. Let me go, feel my way.

I crawl across on all fours so I don't run into any basement thing like the furnace. Fuzziness under my palms. Is it Mrs. H.'s carpet?

I know it's not the basement, but the basement is here. I feel it. Cold and musty and—here's the wall. I stand up, feel for the switch. Where's . . . here it is—*Click!*

The light is so bright, it hurts my eyes, but I'm so glad, so glad, so glad. This is my room, Charlie's room, in Mrs. H.'s house. Mrs. H. says so. I leave the light on, and I lie back on the bed, keeping my eyes open. There's the window, there's the picture of the owl; there's the bookcase filled with books. Everything's here where it belongs in my room in Mrs. H.'s house. I'm never closing my eyes again. I'm keeping away the basement, keeping away the *ihmmmmm.*

Keeping it away, keeping it away . . .

I wake up again, and the room is filled with sunlight. The basement is gone. The smell of bacon steals under my door, and I know Mrs. H. is downstairs cooking it. She's cooking it for Ambrose and for me.

For me.

Ha-ha. For Ambrose and *me.*

---

# CHAPTER SEVENTEEN

"Hi, Aaron. It's Charlie."

"Hi, Charlie. How's it going?"

"All right. My foster mother showed me how to call you."

"Easy, isn't it?"

"Yeah, but I still can't figure out how come I can hear you if you're as far away as Mrs. H. says. You're not shouting or anything."

"Most people don't understand telephones. They just use them without thinking about how they work. After you pick up on your reading, you can look for books that'll tell you those things."

"Books. Well, I'm learning the alphabet again."

"That's a start, Charlie. You'll be really reading soon."

"What are you learning?"

Aaron groans. "Something called algebra. I don't like it much. It has to do with numbers."

"Like counting? My foster brother—Ambrose—has been doing some of that with me."

"Yeah, kinda. You'll see."

Talking on the phone is hard because I can't see Aaron's face.

"How's your arm, Aaron?"

"OK, mostly. I'll be out of the cast soon."

"Still going trick-or-treating on Thanksgiving?"

Aaron laughs. "I can't. My family's going away that week-end."

"Going away?"

"To see my grandparents in Buffalo. That's a city pretty far away. Cold there."

"Will you come back?"

"For sure. We're visiting; that's all."

"I'm glad you're coming back, Aaron."

"Me, too."

# CHAPTER EIGHTEEN

A soccer game's going on across the street. That's what Mrs. H. says it is. Girls with their hair pulled back in what Mrs. H. calls ponytails kick a white-and-black ball all over the place. Sometimes it rolls into the street, and I can get a pretty good look at whoever's getting it. So many girls.

A whole bunch of them chase the ball. They fall down, then get up and run some more. Sometimes they make each other fall down. That's not very nice. If I was closer, maybe I could figure out why they're doing this.

I catch Mrs. H. coming up the stairs with some clean clothes for me. "They chase a ball up and down the grass," I say. "Why?"

She places my shirts and pants on the step outside my room and joins me at the window. "There are two teams playing," she explains.

"Teams." Aaron's on a team.

"Two groups. One group is wearing red shirts; the other is wearing yellow. Do you see that?"

I nod.

"The red team is trying to kick the ball into that net on the other side of the field. The yellow team tries to stop them."

"Why? That's mean."

"No, it's not. They're probably even friends, some of

them. But the girls on the yellow team want to kick the ball into the other net. The team that does it the most wins."

I think about it. "But why?" I ask. "Why does it matter? Why doesn't the red team just give the ball to the yellow team? Why can't each team have its own ball?"

"Because then it's not a game," says Mrs. H. "You want to go over and watch? They won't mind."

I look across to the field. But it's outside. So far away. *Ihmm-ihmm!* Six spider basses away. Brrr. Much better to watch from here. *Ihmm!*

"No, thanks," I say, but I stay at the window.

# CHAPTER NINETEEN

---

"Aren't you afraid?" I ask.

"Nope." Ambrose picks up his backpack from the living-room floor and throws it over his shoulders. It hurts my shoulder to see him do that. "It's only down the street. Want to come with me until the bus comes? It's easy."

I shake my head. I could never go there. Oh, oh! Seven basses play.

"You'll come some other day," Ambrose says. He raises his voice. "Mrs. H.! I'm le-eav-i-i-ing!"

I hear the kitchen door swing open, and here's Mrs. H. "Wait." She's got a brown paper bag she's holding out to Ambrose. "You forgot your lunch. Turkey and cheese."

"With an apple and some cookies?"

She smiles and gives the bag to him. "Only the best for our Ambrose."

Ambrose drops his backpack and unzips one of the pockets before placing his lunch inside. Zip! and it's back over his shoulders. *Twinge!* Goes my shoulder. I wonder if I'll have a backpack someday. I'd have to put it on another way. I rub the twingy place.

"What's the matter, Charlie?" Ambrose asks. "Your shoulder hurt?"

"No." I drop my arm so my hand is hanging loose. Nothing wrong with my shoulder no matter what the X-ray said. It's fine.

Ambrose gets a hug from Mrs. H. before leaving the house. I watch from the living-room window as he walks to the bus stop. How can he just do that? But I see other children. They do it, too—walk toward the end of the street like it doesn't matter. Ambrose runs to catch up with one of them. He and his friend walk together the rest of the way to the corner. In a minute, I see the nose of a big yellow bus. It turns and pauses between me and the bus stop. I hate this part because I can't see Ambrose anymore. How do we know he's all right if we can't see him?

When the bus goes on, no one is left, and nothing shows they were ever there. I look up at Mrs. H. next to me, and she's smiling.

"Aren't you worried about Ambrose?" I ask. "Something could happen to him."

"He's fine," she answers. "I know just where he's going and who he's going to see and pretty much what he's going to do. Nothing to worry about."

"But how do you know, really?"

"It's something you learn."

We turn again to the living room, and I sit on the bottom step while Mrs. H. walks back to the kitchen.

There's a lady coming. A teacher. I'm not sure what a teacher is, even though Mrs. H. told me, even though Ambrose told me.

Someone to show you how to read or work with numbers? I don't get it. How do you do that?

"You'll see," said Mrs. H., when I asked her. "The teacher's very nice. Her name is Mrs. West."

I push my back against the next step and slide my bottom up onto it. I do that again. And again. I move up a bunch of steps while I'm waiting, and Mrs. West still isn't here. I can see the living room and the front door between the banister posts if I duck my head. I don't duck my head. I push onto the next step.

The doorbell rings, and I go back to the last step where I can see. I have to see who it is before I come down. You never really know who's going to be at the front door. Mrs. H. hurries through the living room and opens the door. "Mrs. West? Come on in."

I see her. A lady—a very skinny lady with a high voice and long, black hair that seems to ripple down her back—comes into the living room. She's carrying a cloth bag over one shoulder and tossing that black hair over the other. She's got dark red—really dark red—lips. I don't like them. They look like the spider.

"Charlie?" Mrs. H. looks at me through the posts, but I move my eyes so she can't see them. "Come on down, Charlie, and meet Mrs. West."

But I don't want to come down. Mrs. West has a black-red mouth, and it makes me feel funny in my stomach. She's scary, and she's going to hurt me.

"Charlie?" says Mrs. H.

"Charlie?" repeats the new lady, smiling through those awful lips.

They're both looking at me. I'm not looking at them, but I know they're looking at me. I wish I'd gone all the way up the stairs into my room. I wish I could have climbed even higher so they couldn't find me at all. But there is no place to go, so I just sit here.

I know there's no spider, there never was a spider, but if there is, she's here behind those awful lips.

Mrs. H. says, "Excuse me," and she strides to the bottom of the steps. I look at her with the tops of my eyes. "Charlie, what's wrong?"

There's plenty wrong, I want to say. I'm living in a house that isn't mine. I'm wearing clothes that aren't mine. Everything is different and scary. People tell me I have to start learning things that I don't want to learn, and now someone's here to work with me, and she's scary.

I don't say anything, feeling just as sad and scared as you can feel. *Ihmm-ma-ihmm.*

Mrs. H. comes up and squeezes next to me on the steps. "What's wrong?" she whispers. The flower stuff in her hair surrounds me, and I breathe it in to keep as much of it as I can. The smell helps push back the basement walls I feel closing in on me. The spider basses get quieter. *Ihm-ihm.*

I sneak another glance at Mrs. West through the posts. Her mouth is in a frown. I whisper back. "I don't like Mrs. West."

"Why not?"

"Her mouth—it's—" How can I explain this? "Her mouth—" I cover my eyes with my hands, then bring them down my cheeks. "She's scary. Why does she have lips like that?"

Mrs. H. looks past me to Mrs. West. She laughs, but I don't see what's funny. "It's all right, Charlie. Mrs. West is wearing lipstick, that's all. That's something ladies wear to look pretty."

I turn to see Mrs. H.'s mouth. "You aren't wearing any, and you're pretty." And Mrs. West isn't.

She smiles. "You're sweet," she says. "No, I gave up all that stuff when my husband died. Would you like me to ask Mrs. West to take off her lipstick? I bet she wouldn't mind. If she took it off, her lips would probably be the same color as yours or mine."

Should I say yes? But that might make Mrs. West mad. I better not.

"Can you stay with me?" I ask Mrs. H. "Just for a while. If you stay with me, I can come down."

"Sure, Charlie." She starts to stand up.

"And you won't let anything bad happen?"

"I promise."

So I stand up, too, and fall right down the stairs. I don't stop until I hit the bottom. "Oh!"

"Charlie!" *Clumpity-clumpity!* Mrs. H. is running down after me.

Mrs. West gets to me first. "Are you all right?" she asks. Her eyebrows are up like Jackie's at the hospital. "Did you hit your head?"

But I sit up laughing. I say to Mrs. H., "Maybe Ambrose is right about the steps." My shoulder hurts, but I can't help laughing even though it makes my shoulder hurt more. I'm always so careful about my shoulder, and here I fall like that and land right on it. That's funny, but my shoulder hurts bad, and I can't help holding it. Father said not to hold it, but it hurts a lot, and he's not here.

"You hurt your shoulder, Charlie?" Mrs. H.'s voice is anxious. Her eyebrows are up, too. She's thinking about the X-ray, I know.

I shake my head and make myself take my hand away from my shoulder. I can't talk about my shoulder. I know Father's not here, but—

Mrs. H. leads me to the sofa. "Let me see it."

I pull up my shirt and sweatshirt so she can look. Mrs. West stays over by the staircase like she thinks she's not supposed to see this part. I know there won't be anything for Mrs. H. to find, but she studies my shoulder for a long time before she says, "OK," and I pull my shirts down again.

Mrs. H. is looking at me thoughtfully. "Is your shoulder really all right, Charlie?"

"It'll be fine in a minute," I answer. I rub the soreness. It will be fine. It always is. I just have to remember to be careful.

"You tell me if it's still bothering you later, OK?" asks Mrs. H. "We don't have to wait to have that surgery if it's really bothering you."

I nod my head, but I won't tell her. My father wouldn't like me to talk about it. He wouldn't like me to talk about anything with Mrs. H. or anybody, but I know this is one of those things I really should never talk about. I'm not sure why, but I am sure. "It feels better," I say.

Mrs. H. nods briskly at me. Then she looks over at Mrs. West. "I think we can get started," she says.

Mrs. West comes over and takes a chair on the other side of the coffee table. She smiles at me through those ugly lips while she takes off her coat, but I remember her face from when I fell. I think she's all right. I'm glad that Mrs. H. takes a place on the sofa next to me, but I think Mrs. West is pro-o-bably all right.

"Okay, Charlie," she says. She roots in her bag and pulls out some cards. "Let's see if you can tell me these colors."

Blue, red, black, white, yellow, orange, green, purple, maroon. I tell her all of them.

"Can you put the maroon one away?" I ask. "I really hate maroon," I say. I don't mention the father—I mean the spider. The spider, the spider. That's what it was, not Father. *Ihmm-ihmm*. But that whole thing was a bad dream. A hallucination, Dr. Leidy said. There was no spider. I just remember her; that's all. I'd like to forget her.

"Really?" she asks. "Which one's your favorite?"

"Green. The color of leaves."

Mrs. West puts all the cards away. I guess we're finished with them. She asks me to show her how high I can count. Then I remember something Ambrose said last night.

"One, two, skip a few, a hundred."

Mrs. West stares at me a moment, then laughs. "OK, wise guy," she says.

I feel unsure. What's a wise guy? I look at Mrs. H.

"She means you're being a little fresh," Mrs. H. tells me. She's staring at me, I know, because she thinks this isn't the kind of thing I do. She's right. I don't feel—I'm nervous. But I remember Mrs. H. laughed when Ambrose said it.

"That's all right, Mrs. Harrigan," says Mrs. West. "I can see he's only joking."

Joking. Yes. That's it. So it's all right. I remember the next thing Ambrose said. He said a hundred is a real high number, and then he counted all the way up to it for me. It took a long time, and Mrs. H. was waiting for him to finish before she made him take his bath. She wanted him to say it faster, I think, so he'd get into the bathtub and get ready for bed.

But I don't think *a hundred* means anything. I can picture five things or three things or two things, but a hundred things? How can that mean anything? What can it look like? But Ambrose says when I was learning to read with Mother, I probably knew about a hundred, too. Maybe, but I don't remember it.

Mrs. West says, "I'm impressed. Now, let's see how well you write some of those numbers." She hands me a pad with a pencil. "Show me one to ten."

I take a deep breath and try to remember what Ambrose showed me. The clock in my living room had a different kind of numbers, and for some reason, I can only think of those. Will they be good enough?

I write *I, II, III, IV, V, VI, VII, VIII, IX, X.* Then I stop. She said one to ten.

Mrs. West takes the pad back to look at what I've done. "Roman numerals," she says. "You're ahead of most kids with those."

I am? I'm ahead in some way?

She hands back the pad. "Let's see them the other way."

I feel real small, like a piece of dirt with grass stuck to it. Real small.

I look at Mrs. H. What do I do? I whisper in her ear. "I can't remember the ones Ambrose was showing me."

"Just tell her, Charlie," she whispers back. "She knows you need to learn a lot of stuff. That's why she's here."

Mrs. West's eyes are going back and forth between Mrs. H. and me. I can tell she doesn't understand.

I give her back her pad. "I can't," I say.

"Can't what?" Mrs. West asks.

Mrs. H. pats my back. "Tell her," she urges me.

"Can't you?"

Mrs. H. shakes her head. "Some things we have to do for ourselves," she says. "This one's yours."

So I take a deep breath.

"I can't write," I tell Mrs. West. "Ambrose is teaching me the alphabet and numbers again, but I can't remember them this morning. It's all empty where I try to think of it."

Mrs. West stares at me again. "You aren't kidding this time, are you?"

A hundred basses. *Ihmmmmm* . . .

I look at my lap and shake my head. "No." Yucky. Like grass stuck in poop. That's what Ambrose calls the b.m.'s. *Poop.* There's a worse word for it, he told me, but he wouldn't say it with Mrs. H. walking back and forth out in the hall with laundry. *Later,* he whispered. Then we forgot. Maybe there's a word even worse than Ambrose's word, and maybe one even worse than that.

And that's how I feel. Like a piece of grass stuck in worst-word poop.

I almost expect Mrs. West to put on her coat and leave.

She can't work with someone who can't even remember his numbers. That's what she'll say. I can see she thinks everybody's supposed to be able to write numbers. Probably she thinks that about reading. What would Father say if she told him that? I would tell Mrs. West not to tell him that. But she's never going to see him anyway and—

"Well," says Mrs. West. She reaches again into that bag of hers and pulls out a big, blue book. She carries it around to the sofa and sits on the other side of me from Mrs. H. "Then I'll just have to show you." She opens the cover of the book. Inside is a bunch of writing. Her voice rises as she points to a straight line. "One."

"One," I say, just the same way. Now that I see it, I remember. Just like Ambrose was showing me. Sure.

She points to a curvy thing, and her voice rises again. "Two."

Mine does, too. "Two." Got it.

"Three."

"Three." I think of what comes next, and before Mrs. West can go on, I say the next number, the one I learned from Dr. Leidy: "GO!"

# CHAPTER TWENTY

I'm sitting on the bedroom carpet looking at one of the books when Mrs. H. comes up the stairs with my laundry. I close the book and shove it back on the shelf right away when I see her.

"You may look at that," she says. She places the folded clothes on my bed. "My son won't mind." She pulls out one of the other books. It has a big, colorful picture on the front cover. "This was one of his favorites, *Time of Wonder*." Her face takes on a softness it sometimes gets when she talks about her son. "We pretty much had this one memorized."

"Father says I'll be bad if I read," I tell her. "He'd be angry if he saw me looking at books."

She opens *Time of Wonder*. I see more pictures inside. "This book," she says, "was written for children, just like *The Cat in the Hat* was." She makes a sweeping gesture at the bookcases. "Most of these were."

"But Father—"

"Your father is a sick man," she says. "That's why he told you those things. But he was wrong. It's very important for children to learn to read. The earlier the better."

"But Father isn't sick. I was the one who was sick. Real sick."

"No." She shakes her head. "Not that kind of sick."

Father is sick? He never looked sick to me. Of course, his

face gets red like the spider. That's when he's mad. Is that what Mrs. H. means?

"You'll understand one of these days," says Mrs. H. "You'll understand and it will all make sense. Or most of it will. And the stuff that doesn't, you'll at least feel better about." She gives me the book in her hand. "Books are good. You'll find out."

But when I look inside, it's still all black marks except for the pictures. Then a couple of the marks come together to mean something.

"Hey." I point. "*Is—I—S—is*." I look farther down the page, pointing. "Is, is, is." Clear places that break up a big blur.

Mrs. H. claps her hands. "Wonderful," she says.

I see something else. "*The—T—H—E—the*. I remember. That's the first word in *The Cat in the Hat*, Mrs. H. See? It looks the same."

Mrs. H. claps again. I feel real proud.

"Hey, Ambrose!" I carry the book downstairs to the living room. Mrs. H. is right behind me. "Look!" And I show him some *the*'s, and some *is*'s.

He looks at me from the toy cars he's pushing around on the carpet and grins. Then he points to another group of marks that aren't just marks anymore. "I bet you can tell me that one, too."

I look at it, squinting and trying the marks—the letters. "*A—nn-d. And*."

Ambrose jumps up and down yelling, and Mrs. H. doesn't tell him to stop. She just claps to the yells.

"I knew you could read," says Ambrose. He's out of breath, and his smile shows all of his teeth. "I knew you could do it. Anyone who can climb those stairs can sure read. I knew it all along."

I don't know what the connection is, but maybe there is one.

We sit on the sofa, and Ambrose reads me *Time of Wonder*. Every now and then, Ambrose points to a word and waits while I try it. Sometimes I get it, and sometimes Ambrose has to help me. I see Mrs. H. watching from across the room, and I think she's holding her breath.

"Wow, Charlie," she says. "You're amazing."

She leaves the room, and Ambrose picks up *The Cat in the Hat* from the coffee table. We read that together, too. I get more words this time, and Ambrose says that's because it's an easier book and because he's read it to me before.

Well, here's what I think about *The Cat in the Hat*. It's dumb. I don't tell Ambrose that's what I think because he likes it. He laughs. But I don't think it's funny. It's dumb. It's worse than dumb.

This mother goes out and leaves her children all alone with the door unlocked. That's real dumb. Then a cat that's real tall and can't really be a cat comes in—just walks into the house and messes everything up!

The children are all afraid of what their mother will say when she comes back. Why are they afraid of her? It's their father they should worry about. The mother shouldn't have left them alone. She should never have left the door un-locked. She must have known that. Why didn't the children hide from the cat? Didn't they know about basements and punishment? Why weren't they scared? And what did the father say?

I was really worried about that the first time I heard it, and I could hardly listen to the end, but then there was no father. No father at all. Like a big, blank spot at the end of the story.

"Why isn't there a father?" I asked Ambrose.

Ambrose told me, "Not every house has a father."

"But it's supposed to be—"

He interrupted. "There's no father in this house."

That's true. Mrs. H. says that Mr. H. died a long time ago. But it still doesn't make sense.

After we finish reading *The Cat in the Hat* this time, Ambrose points to the picture of Thing One. "That's what I went as for Halloween this year," he tells me.

Then I tell him about Aaron missing Halloween and how we were going to go trick-or-treating on Thanksgiving.

"Ha-ha-ha-ha," laughs Ambrose. "That would have been funny."

Thanksgiving is in a few days, and I'm thinking how I'm glad I'm not going trick-or-treating with Aaron, after all. How could I? There's always the outside between me and—and anything. You go out in it, and someone takes the air away. The outside slaps you in the face like a stinging wind, and no matter how you gulp the air, you can't get any.

Going outside—brrr! I didn't know this would happen, but when I go outside, I feel awful. Every time. So I don't go out unless Mrs. H. says I absolutely have to.

Today I absolutely have to. Today's a counseling day with

Dr. Leidy at the center next to the hospital. I hate going. Dr. Leidy keeps asking me questions about my parents and how I feel about them. I don't like answering her questions. Besides, why can't she come here? But Mrs. H. says she just can't, period.

OK. But why do I have to go there? I'm safe here. Isn't that the main thing? I'm safe. That's all I want. Why can't the grown-ups leave it at that?

The box Mrs. H. carried up to my room the first day had all the clothes in it that I'll ever need. She gives me all kinds of good food. Mrs. West comes from the school almost every day to teach me, and I'm safe. That's the main thing.

Safe.

That is really the main thing.

Well . . .

There are other things. Like why can't I see my mother? And how come I want to see Father even if he did bad things to me? Even if I'm scared I might see him? I want to see Mother and Father so bad. And I want everything to be good so we can live together again. Why can't it be possible to be with them and be safe at the same time? I wish someone would make that happen.

*Ihmmmmm . . .*

But I don't want to talk to Dr. Leidy about this stuff. Father would say it's none of her business. That's what I tell Mrs. H. right now.

"Yes, it is." Mrs. H. has come into the room with my coat in her hands. "Come on, Charlie. We don't want to be late."

I do. I want to be more than late.

I edge behind the sofa and slide behind it to the floor. I like it here. There's room for me and nothing else. The solid wall against my side feels good. Pushes aside the basses. The basement. The basses.

The sofa moves away, and there's Mrs. H. staring down at me, still holding my coat. Ambrose is staring at me, too. He's got an apple next to his mouth, but he's not eating it. He's only looking down at me with those big, brown eyes, not saying anything.

"Charlie, you have to go," says Mrs. H.

I get up. "But why? I'm fine here."

"Charlie, do you trust me?"

All grown-ups get to asking me that. "Sure," I say. "I guess. You're real nice to me, making pea soup with hot-dog chunks and stuff."

That makes her smile. "Well, if I'm so nice, why am I making you see Dr. Leidy?"

"I don't know," I mutter.

Over the steady hum of the basses, I take the coat and put it on. Before the doorway, I stop. "Is the car unlocked, Mrs. H.?" I ask.

She nods.

When she opens the front door, I carefully look all around, then race for the car. Run—*open door*—INSIDE—*DONE*!

I click the seat belt on tight and crunch low in the backseat. My heart is racing, and my ears feel funny. *Ihmmmmm!* Basement, basement, basement crushing me. I can't breathe! *Ihmm-ihmm-ihmmm!*

After what seems like forever, Ambrose and Mrs. H. get

into the car, too. Mrs. H. hands me a brown paper bag, and I put it open over my face. In a minute, I feel better, the basement pulls back, and I take the bag off again.

Mrs. H. is looking at me from the front seat. "OK, now?" she asks.

"You looked funny with that bag over your face," says Ambrose, laughing. Then he picks it up from the seat between us and pulls it over his face. "Ha-ha-ha-ha." His voice is muffled. "Do I look funny, too, Charlie? Ha-ha-ha."

"You always look funny," I say, and that makes him laugh harder.

He drops the bag, still laughing. Then he pulls on the sides of his eyes and sticks out his tongue. "How about that?" he asks. "Is that funny, too?"

I make another face back. "How about mine?" Then we're both laughing too hard to make faces.

Mrs. H. is silent up in the driver's seat, but I notice we're already at the traffic light, and I stop laughing.

Dr. Leidy, ugh. I like Dr. Leidy, but ugh, anyway.

I have to go outside again to see her. No, she won't come out to the car. I asked that the last time.

Mrs. H. parks in the center's lot, and I wait until she gets out before I get out. Take a real good look around. No Father. No Mother.

I know they aren't supposed to see me, but couldn't they sometime just happen to be here when I come? Coming from a haircut or buying stamps? Father does that, I know.

My hand is still on the car door. I look up at Mrs. H. She's tucking the paper bag into her coat pocket. "May I run?"

She shakes her head. "Not this time, Charlie. There's too much traffic in the lot, and we couldn't park any closer today."

The center of the basses' quiet tone hardens. *Erriihmmm!* I take a deep breath and grab Mrs. H.'s hand. I hold tight to her hand, but she doesn't say anything about that. She understands, and I'm glad. She takes Ambrose's hand on her other side, and we walk. The distance to the door is forever. By the time we get there, my ears feel funny again, and my chest hurts from all the pounding. We go inside, and I take the paper bag out of Mrs. H.'s pocket. I sit on the floor and put the bag over my face.

The basement's almost gone when I hear, "Charlie?" It's Dr. Leidy. I take the bag away and give it back to Mrs. H. I might need it when we leave. Then I follow Dr. Leidy, and I know she's going to ask about the bag.

The bag and the basement. I won't tell her about the basses.

*Ihmmmmm!*

# CHAPTER TWENTY-ONE

It's different talking to Dr. Leidy here. For some reason, when I was sick in the hospital, I could tell her stuff. But here, everything is too stiff; the carpet is too new. Or something. I don't want to tell her anything she asks about.

Between us, a cloth-covered table holds cars and people the size of my fingers. I look at them instead of her.

"You can play with those if you want," she says. "That's why I have them." That's what she's told me on other visits, but I wait until she says it again in case the rules have changed.

So I'm pushing a green car when Dr. Leidy asks, "How is it living with Mrs. H.?"

I think about that question. Look at it from all sides the same as I look at the car with its pretend doors that can't open. The question seems like a safe one to answer. But how do I know she won't tell Father what I say? And I'll be with Father again sometime, so I can't answer. Father will be angry.

"Do you like Mrs. H.?"

I still don't answer.

Dr. Leidy's eyebrows come almost together, and she lifts something from the table at her elbow. I cringe. It's a piece of paper.

Dr. Leidy speaks. "I think you're afraid to talk with me, Charlie. Am I right?"

I wish I hadn't cringed.

"Please answer, Charlie. Am I right?"

I nod, but I don't say anything. I push that car and push that car.

"Why are you afraid? Do you think I might do something to hurt you?"

I pick up the green car, rolling it between my palms, feeling the hard edges against my skin. It's very important that I feel the hard edges. "Maybe," I mutter, over the basses.

Dr. Leidy nods. "I understand. But think about this. I'm never going to hurt you. I don't want to. But just in case I did hurt you, do you know how much trouble I'd be in?"

I feel my eyes get wide. "You? How would you be in trouble? You're a grown-up."

"Grown-ups can get into trouble. Think about that a minute."

I do. But it doesn't work. Grown-ups? I look at Dr. Leidy, not getting it at all.

"Grown-ups—" I give up and shrug my good shoulder.

"Grown-ups, yes." Dr. Leidy adds, "Grown-ups can be in trouble. Your mother and father are grown-ups. Don't you think they are in trouble for keeping you in the basement?"

I stand up and walk around my chair. I walk around it three times, before I sit down again. I put down the green car. Then I pull on my fingers and my ears, my hair. *ERR-ihmm-ma-ihmm-ma-ihmm-ma.* So loud, so loud.

"What's wrong?" Dr. Leidy asks.

I don't want to say anything. Then I blurt it out. "What you said! My father, my father—everyone says he did something wrong, but I'm the one who was bad. I was being *punished*!

Why do people keep getting that wrong? It was me who was bad. I'm the one who should be in trouble, not Father or Mother."

Dr. Leidy waits a minute before answering. "Charlie." Her voice is quiet. So are the basses. I don't like it when voices get too quiet. Scary. Father's voice would get real quiet when he was going to send me down to the basement.

Where is Dr. Leidy going to send me? Does she have a basement here somewhere? But she thinks my parents were wrong to send me to the one at home.

"Charlie, a father or mother might punish a child for something. He might punish by taking away television privileges, or by sending him to his room for an hour, or something like that. But a parent who keeps his son in the basement—"

"No, no, no!" I yell. "Don't say this!"

Dr. Leidy continues, "—that parent is doing something wrong. He isn't punishing his child. He's hurting his child. There's a word for that. Do you know what it is?"

I shake my head.

"*Abuse.* Charlie, you have been abused by your parents if they did those things to you. That means they hurt you, that they mistreated you. And that would get them into trouble."

"Wait." Conflict is pulling my brain apart. "It was punishment. That's all it was."

Dr. Leidy is shaking her head. "A person could call it punishment, but that wouldn't make it so."

"And besides, Mother never did anything to me. She never hurt me at all."

Dr. Leidy stops shaking her head. "Your mother never hurt you?"

"No, she didn't. She never would."

"Did someone hurt you, Charlie?"

I don't want to say it.

Dr. Leidy waits.

"It wasn't Mother." That's all I can say.

*Ihmm-ma-ihmm-ma-ihmmm . . .*

The room is so quiet, I can hear the air moving, can hear my breath.

*Ihmm-ma-ihmm . . .*

So quiet even though the spider basses hum. Through them I ask, "If I say it, will that make it easier to go outside?"

But the basement is everywhere. *Ihmmmmm . . .*

"It could help."

I pull on my ears again. "Can I ask you a question first?"

*Ihmm-ma-ihmm-ma-ihmm . . .*

"Sure."

"Are you going to tell Father what I say?" *Maa-ihmm . . .* He'll put me back in the basement with those crumbly walls all around. Will I ever get another chance to go back up-stairs? *Maa-ihmmmmm . . .*

"Charlie, a large part of what my job is has to do with keeping you safe. The law says that I have to tell the authorities when I find that a client has been hurt by a grown-up. As long as you're a child, that's the law. And your parents could find out what I report. I can't prevent that."

Oh, no! I'm never saying anything else! *Father!*

"But this is all about keeping you as safe as possible," says

Dr. Leidy. "So the right people can be there to protect you."

"I'll be protected?"

"As much as it can be done. Part of keeping you safe is letting people know how you've been hurt. Then they know what protection you need."

*Ma-ihmm-ma—*

I'm still pulling on my ears, but I'm going to say it. I'm not really, really sure about Dr. Leidy and all those people she'll have to tell, but I'm going to try. Father? I think about how I hid behind Dr. Leidy when we left the hospital. I'll try.

*MA-IHMM-MA-IHMM!*

"My father hurt me." I can hardly hear my own voice over the spider's tone. It's so loud, so loud, I hold my ears. I can't hear Dr. Leidy's next question because I'm holding them. Something bad is about to happen. A hundred basses blast my head. Then not a hundred. Then ten, then five.

I drop my hands.

"What happened?" Dr. Leidy asks.

"I don't know," I say, because I don't. I wish I did. "It just got really loud inside my head."

Almost no basses. Why?

"OK, now?"

"I think so." Cautiously, I look around the room, at the door. The room is empty except for Dr. Leidy and me. No Father. No Father at all.

"What? No Father?" Dr. Leidy asks.

Oh. I said that out loud. "He's not here," I say. "It felt like he was here for a minute. But he's not. He's really not."

"No, Charlie, he's really not."

# CHAPTER TWENTY-TWO

"Hi, Aaron."

"Hey, Charlie. Guess what? I'm out of my cast."

"Great. Can you play soccer, yet?"

"Naw. I still have to be careful. I could break the arm again. I definitely don't want to do that. Then I might have to have surgery."

"I have to have that on my shoulder sometime. My shoulder got broken a long time ago, and it didn't heal right."

"Well, that's lousy. When do you have to do that?"

"I don't know. When it hurts bad enough, I guess."

"Hmm. Hey, you want to see my team play? Maybe Mrs. H. would drive you to the field on Saturday. Wanna come? We'll sit in the stands and cheer and eat pizza."

"With orange soda?"

"Sure, if you want. You wanna come?"

I don't answer.

"Charlie?"

"Oh, well, Aaron." My voice is low. "Something happened. I don't know what it is, but I can't go outside."

"Mrs. H. grounded you, but you don't know what for?"

"*Grounded?*"

"Never mind. You're not being punished?"

"No. I just can't go outside. It makes me feel sick and

awful. It never happened before, but—so I don't go outside unless Mrs. H. makes me."

"That's the worst," says Aaron. "You gotta be able to go outside. Otherwise how are you ever going to play soccer or anything else?"

I shake my head.

"Charlie, are you there?"

"Yeah. I was shaking my head, but you couldn't see me."

"Charlie, you're gonna try, aren't you?"

"I—"

"Promise me you're gonna try."

"Sure, Aaron. I'll try."

"Great, Charlie. We'll get you playing soccer yet."

# CHAPTER TWENTY-THREE

It's Thanksgiving. I can't figure out what's going on. Mrs. H.'s son Ellis is here from another city. So's his wife, Mona, and baby daughter. Her name is Clarice. Ambrose calls her licorice because he thinks Clarice sounds like licorice. I asked him what licorice is, and he said black candy, so I don't know. I haven't seen that.

But the baby's crying, and Ellis is pacing with her while Mona and Mrs. H. are talking in the kitchen. It sounds like arguing to me, but Ellis says they're just talking loudly because the mixer's on and so's the dryer.

Mona comes out. "Your turn," she says to Ellis. "You get to chop the veggies." She sits in a chair, and he gives her Clarice. Clarice quiets right down. Smiling, Ellis watches Clarice and Mona together for a moment before leaving the room.

Clarice is happy. She isn't crying anymore, and Ambrose and I can go back to playing Sorry! You can't play games when someone is crying.

Sorry!'s an all-right game, I guess, but I can't read the cards. Ambrose can't read all of them, either, but he knows what they mean.

Well, I can read the word *sorry* now. *Is, sorry, the, and, at, cat, hat.* The list is getting longer. Pretty soon I'll be able to read sentences, I bet. I can read my name: Charlie Porter. I feel like only the *Charlie* part is right. Mrs. H. says my name really is Charles. *Charles Alan Porter.* I tell her she's wrong, but she acts sure. How come she knows my name better than me? But I'm getting to know what *Charles Alan Porter* looks like, too. The words. I guess I know what I look like. But it's kind of strange.

Since the hospital, Mrs. H. cut my hair. It's real short now. Mrs. H. calls it a crew cut. I don't look the way I remember from before the basement. Skinny, OK, but there's something else. My jaw is longer or something. Mrs. H. says I'm growing up. She says I'll have a beard and a deep voice before I know it. That would be funny.

Mrs. H. comes out from the kitchen. "Charlie and Ambrose, I need your help setting the table."

We push the game board under the coffee table and follow Mrs. H. In the kitchen everything smells great, and there's food everywhere I look.

"Are more people coming?" I ask. "There's so much food."

Ellis laughs. "I hope so," he says. "Mom can't be expecting just us to eat all that."

"Now, you hush," says Mrs. H. "Nothing wrong with a few leftovers. Besides, we are having a little more company."

She looks down at Ambrose and smiles. "Your brother Ross called to say he could come, after all."

Ambrose drops the forks he's holding. He acts like he doesn't know they fell even though they crash so noisily onto the floor. He just stares at Mrs. H.

"Ross?" He whispers it. "Ross is coming?"

Mrs. H. smiles even more widely. "He sure is. Isn't that a nice surprise?"

Ambrose jumps up into the air, laughing and hooting. He laughs so hard he falls down. Then he gets up and jumps some more.

Mrs. H. opens the back door and shoos Ambrose outside. "Run around the house three times, Ambrose."

Ambrose stops on the mat. "You come, too," he says to me. His hand is out.

Brrr. I don't move.

"Come on," Ambrose says again. "It's not so much fun alone. And *Ross* is coming. You *have* to come."

Mrs. H. is silent, still holding the door, but she is watching me. Ellis looks up from his chopping. "Oh, heck." He puts down his knife. I see his apron with the faded flowers on it. "If *Ross* is coming, we *all* have to run around the house three times."

He pushes his mother onto the doorsill.

"But," she starts, but Ellis guides her onto the big top step behind Ambrose. Ambrose turns so I can see his wide smile.

Now Ellis takes my hand, and I don't have time to think about it. Out we go, turning right to follow Ambrose and Mrs. H. down the concrete steps. I slide the fingers of my other hand along the wall of the house as we go. It's cold and so is the air but nobody else cares. I want to run back inside, but Ellis has my hand. I know I'm safe with Ellis and Mrs. H. I'm safe I'm safe I'm safe. Why am I so scared if I'm safe?

"On your mark," shouts Ambrose, "get set, go!"

As soon as we start, Ellis drops my hand. He stays with me for the first while, but once we get around the side of the house, he takes off.

I try keeping up with Ellis in his flapping apron, but he's awful fast. So's Ambrose. I stay even with Mrs. H. We're running, running. I see the front walk, now the bushes in the side yard. Now we go past the backdoor steps. Running, running. Front walk, bushes, backdoor steps.

I'm alone. I stop and turn around. Mrs. H. is sitting on the bottom step. She's waving her hands at me to go on because she's out of breath.

Go on alone? But then Ambrose and Ellis, laughing and shouting, tear around the far side. Ellis stops with Mrs. H., but Ambrose keeps going.

"Come on!" he shouts, as he passes me, so I run to catch up. Running, running. A cat shoots across the grass. Running, running. A blue car stops in the street. Front walk, bushes, Ambrose shouting. Back door—made it! Made it, made it, made it! Through the cold air! Three times!

Ambrose and I shout and jump while Ellis and Mrs. H. clap from the steps. I wish we could all do it again; it was so much fun. Made it!

The back door opens and Mona comes out with Clarice. "What's going on?" she asks.

She comes down the steps, and Ellis takes Clarice from her. He says a few words to her, but I'm watching his face as he looks at Clarice. It's so soft. Then I look at Mona watching. Then I look at Mrs. H. She's watching, too. All pink and smiling like everything is perfect.

For some reason it jolts my stomach to see this.

I feel like I want Ellis to look at me that way, not at Clarice. But that's not it really. I want Father to look at me that way. I don't remember him ever looking at me like that—like I was just the most perfect thing. And what did Clarice do to make Ellis look at her like that? Nothing. She's asleep. Then why's he so proud and happy?

Mona and Ellis go back inside with Clarice who's still sleeping in the cold air.

Cold. The air is cold. I'm cold. So cold I wouldn't feel a pin stuck in my hand.

I follow without saying anything. I walk past the food in the kitchen, the dining-room table that's partly set for dinner, the coffee table with Sorry! pushed under it.

Huh! Sorry! What's *sorry*?

I keep walking until I reach the steps.

"Charlie?" Ambrose catches me at the bottom. "What's wrong?"

I shake my head. "I don't feel so good."

I start up.

"But you're coming back down, aren't you? It's almost time for dinner. And Ross is coming."

"No," I say. "I just want to lie down."

I finish the climb to my room and pull the quilt over me because I'm so cold. I wish I had two quilts. Four, ten. Maybe ten would be heavy enough.

The quilt gets hot even though I still feel all wrong. It's like I'm cold, but I'm not. I throw off the quilt and get up from the bed to stare out the window. Nothing to see, and I don't care.

Seeing Ellis look so proud of Clarice and loving her so much—why can't I have that, too? Why doesn't my father look at me like that? All of them—Mrs. H., Ellis, Mona, even Clarice. They look at each other like what they have between them is the best thing, the only thing worth having. Like Aaron's dad and Aaron.

And I can't stand it. I wish when I'd been running that I'd run a straight line. I wish I'd run so far so I could never see this. But where would I go in the awful OUTSIDE? And how could I keep from knowing, anyhow?

I run my fingers along the windowsill, feeling the unevenness of wood under the paint. I don't like it here. It's the best I can have, but I don't like it. I want to be back with Father and Mother. I want to be back at the lake house when things were still good. I want things to go some way different from there so they can stay good.

*Knock, knock, knock!*

"Go away," I say.

But the knocks go on. I open the door.

Ambrose.

"Go away."

He looks so sad, but he turns away without answering.

Wait. It's *Ambrose*. He never comes up here. He's afraid of the stairs.

"Ambrose, hold it."

He turns around.

"Why are you up here?" I ask. "You hate the steps."

"I came up because it's important," he answers. "I can come up if it's important."

He walks across the blue carpet and sprawls on my bed. "Hey," he says, "I have a quilt just like this one. I spilled grape juice on mine, though, so it has a stain on these orange stripes." He takes the teddy bear from its spot and holds it against his side.

"What's so important?" I slouch next to him. "Why'd you come up?"

"It's *Thanksgiving*," says Ambrose. "You have to have Thanksgiving."

"I never had one before, so I don't care about it."

"Well, you should start."

"Why? It's all about families being together. If you don't know that, look at Mrs. H. and Ellis and those guys. This is their Thanksgiving. Their family."

"You miss your parents." He doesn't ask. He just says it like it's a fact. Well, it is a fact.

"They won't even let me see Mother," I say. "Why can't I at least see her?"

Ambrose seems to understand.

"They won't let me see my mom, either," says Ambrose. He bounces a little on the bed. "They wouldn't let me see her even after she sent me a box of chocolate-chip cookies. And they were good cookies." His lower lip starts to quiver, and he wipes his eyes on one of the teddy bear's ears. His tears make me feel bad, so I put my arm around his shoulders.

"Why won't they let you see her?" I ask.

"Well . . ." He shifts his eyes away. "She did stuff and I got hurt. She pushed me down the stairs. That's one thing she did."

"That's why you don't like staircases."

"Only long, skinny ones like that one." He points. "Big, wide ones, I don't care."

I thought about what he said. "But why do you want to see her if she did that?"

"Don't you get it?" he asks. "She's my mother. And I know she only lost her temper. She's real nice to me most of the time. She even took me to the zoo, just me, and we stayed all, all afternoon to see the lions because I like lions. And she bought me ice cream, too."

"But she shouldn't ever push you down the stairs," I say, "even if she loses her temper." How could she have done that to Ambrose? Ambrose is a special kid, the way his voice laughs when he talks. Anyone can see that. The way he always thinks the good things—how he knew I could read before I did. Stuff like that. "Even if she loses her temper," I repeat.

Ambrose sighs. "That's what everybody says." His voice isn't laughing now. He looks up at me again. "But see? It's the same way with your mom. She's a nice lady, but she did something bad."

"She didn't do anything bad."

Ambrose stares at me with his mouth open. "But I heard she put you in the basement for a long time. Real long. That's a bad thing."

"My father did that. Mother couldn't help me; that's all."

"Why? She's a grown-up."

I can't think of an answer to that, but I know I'm right. "You don't understand," I say.

"Yeah." He slouches over his knees. "Probably not. People don't understand about my mother, either. Mrs. H. says that's just the way it is. But I get to see Ross sometimes." He sits up straight. "That's the real reason I want you to come downstairs. Ross is coming. We'll all be sad if you stay up here, and *Ross is coming!* We can't be sad when *Ross is coming.*"

I push back and sit against the wall. "No. Thanksgiving is for families. You guys have a good time. I'll feel better up here."

"Families, huh!" shouts Ambrose. "Don't brothers count as family?"

"Sure. You and Ross. Family."

He points at me. "Charlie and me. Family."

"What?"

"Don't you get it, you dope? *We're* brothers. *We're* family."

I'm startled. Then I look at him, and his face makes me smile. Then I start to laugh.

"I forgot," I say. "We're *brothers!*"

"Yeah! And Ellis is our brother, too. All brothers. So it's all family down there, right?"

He cracks me up with that face. "Right."

*Ding-dong!*

Ambrose drops the teddy bear and walks to the top of the stairs. "Hey, Mrs. H.!" he shouts down. "Is that Ross?"

An unfamiliar voice answers. "Where's that Ambrose kid?" The voice is real deep. "Where is that kid?"

Ambrose giggles. "It's Ross," he says. He runs back to the bed and grabs my arm. "Come on, Charlie. Come see Ross. You have to come see Ross."

I still don't want to go downstairs, but I don't have the heart to say no the way Ambrose is looking at me.

On the way down, though, I'm glad I gave in. Ambrose holds my hand tight the whole time, and I can see by how wide his eyes are how scared he is. We take the steps re-e-al slow so he can put both feet on each tread before going on.

"It's always harder going down," he whispers about halfway. He grunts before taking the next step. "I woulda needed someone to help. Good thing for me you changed your mind."

When we get to the bottom, there's Ross—a tall, stretched-out version of Ambrose. Ross lifts Ambrose like he's a baby, and Ambrose doesn't say anything, just hugs Ross around the neck just as hard as I'm smiling.

# CHAPTER TWENTY-FOUR

"Did you have a good Thanksgiving, Charlie?"

"There was so much food, Aaron."

"Did you run around outside after dinner to burn up some of it?"

"We did that before dinner." I explain about Ambrose and Ross.

"Ambrose sounds like a cool kid," says Aaron. "When you come to the soccer game, bring him with you."

"Well—"

"You said you went outside and ran around the house three times."

"Yeah, but—"

"Hey, it's a start. Like the alphabet. You reading anything, yet?"

"I can read most of *The Cat in the Hat*. Mrs. H. or Ambrose helps me with the hard words."

"That's great, Charlie."

"I don't like the story, though," I say. "I don't like the mother."

"It's for little kids, Charlie. They like the cat."

I think about that. "Oh. Well, the cat's funny if you don't worry about the mother."

"Trust me, Charlie. That's a mother not to worry about."

# CHAPTER TWENTY-FIVE

Mrs. West is here. I've already colored in the pictures of boxes with ribbons. I was going to color them all brown, like the box my clothes came in, but she says these are pictures of presents, and presents get wrapped with colored paper. So one is blue, one is yellow, and one I color red with brown stripes. Except I don't like the color the brown makes when it touches the red, so I change the brown to blue, and I push real hard over the ugly color.

"That's good, Charlie," Mrs. West says. "Now I need you to cut those boxes out. On the back of each box is a number. See if you can match that number with the same number in the squares under the picture of the Christmas tree."

I look at the Christmas tree in the picture. I don't understand it. It looks like the pine trees in my old backyard, the backyard with the basement, but those pine trees never had loops and funny balls on them. Just pinecones. I remember what I did under those trees, and it makes me feel bad. *Ihmmm* . . . I shove the basses away so they're just below the line.

It's been a while since I was under those pines, though, so maybe it's rained enough to get rid of it. I hope so.

"Charlie, why did you stop working?" asks Mrs. West. "You're frowning so hard."

I blink and look at her. "Just thinking," I say. I drop my gaze to the Christmas-tree picture again. "I don't understand about the Christmas tree. It looks kind of like a pine tree. I've seen those, but," I go on quickly so she can't ask me about the pine trees I know. "I've never seen one with these things on it. It—I—is this a made-up thing like the Cat in the Hat? I mean cats don't really look like that, and the ones I see cutting across the backyard don't walk on two legs." I stop, not sure how to say what I mean, and Mrs. West doesn't answer. She just stares at me. Did I say something wrong?

Her voice is soft when she finally does speak. "Charlie, oh, my goodness, Charlie." She gets up and leaves me in the kitchen, saying, "I'll be right back," over her shoulder. Her voice sounds funny.

I take the picture of the Christmas tree to the window over the sink. I look from it to the trees and bushes that line the back of Mrs. H.'s yard. None of them looks anything like the picture, but none of them are pines, either.

Then I study the picture again. I decide that the balls and things are kind of like Mrs. West's crayon earrings that she's wearing today. She's already explained earrings to me.

"They're something ladies wear to dress up," she said once. "Some men wear them, too. To look a little fancier."

"The same as lipstick?" I asked.

She nodded vigorously. "The same idea."

So somebody dressed up a pine tree. That's what it means. Why would anyone do that? But why dress up ears, either? Or lips? Aren't they fine the way they are?

I go out into the living room where Mrs. West is talking with Mrs. H. It looks like a serious conversation, but it stops as soon as I come in.

"I figured out the Christmas tree," I announce.

"What do you mean?" asks Mrs. West.

"It's just a pine tree all dressed up," I say. Then I ask them both. "But why would you dress up a tree?"

Mrs. West and Mrs. H. exchange a glance, so I know there's something odd about my question. There's always something odd about my questions. It means there's another gap in what I know.

"I'll be buying a tree this weekend so we can decorate it," says Mrs. H. finally. "Ambrose and I will explain all about Christmas trees and Christmas while we're doing that, OK?"

"Sure," I say. It's no big deal, I figure.

My teacher and I return to the kitchen where she watches me cut out the colored boxes. She's still looking kind of worried.

"It's OK me not knowing about Christmas trees," I tell her. "I didn't know about Thanksgiving or Halloween, either. But I'm learning. Pretty soon I'll be just like a regular kid."

Mrs. West sits back in her chair and laughs. "To tell you the truth, Charlie," she says, "there is no such thing as a regular kid."

And somehow, that makes me glad.

# CHAPTER TWENTY-SIX

"So, how's life treating you?" asks Aaron.

We're talking face-to-face on the living-room sofa this time, not over the phone. He looks bigger than I remember him from the hospital, with darker hair and eyes, too. His shirt is bright with red and blue stripes. It's like someone made all his colors stand out against the quiet air.

"Pretty good," I say. "I'm still getting used to everything."

"I bet you are. You must feel sometimes like you got dropped here from outer space."

I know my face must look like I don't get it again, and Aaron laughs.

"Outer space is what people call where the stars and the sun and the moon are; that's all."

"Oh. Well, you're right. That is exactly how I feel. One day I was living with my parents, and the next—*Bang!*—that part of my life was over."

"Like you woke up from a nightmare by cracking your head on the floor when you fell out of bed."

"That's it," I say. "Everything was different all at once."

"But the nightmare's over. That's the good part."

"The nightmare's over, but sometimes it's hard to remember that."

"Well." Aaron considers. "It was a long nightmare. Why wouldn't it stick to you? After I was hit by that car, I was scared and shook up. The car was long gone and I was safe in the hospital, but I was still scared. And that was a short thing, not like yours."

"But pretty awful."

"Sometimes the feeling of the accident still comes over me—the sound of the tires screeching, the smell of the street, and how it all felt. But not too often now. And when that happens, I just shake my head and think of other things. Like soccer." He grins. "Everybody should think about soccer."

Sounds of the conversation between Aaron's mother and Mrs. H. ride out from the kitchen on the smell of coffee. We're eating cookies and drinking soda. Mine's orange soda and his is just a regular cola.

"Are you playing soccer, yet?" I ask.

He breaks his cookie in two and dunks it in his soda before taking a bite. I wouldn't eat it that way, that's for sure. But I don't like colas, anyway.

"No. Soon, though. Mom and I are on our way to that soccer store I told you about. You want to go with us? Mom says it's all right to ask you. Maybe you'd like to buy a soccer ball."

Go with?

"I—" I'd like to, but the outside—Oh! and *Ihmmmmm!*—I bite my lower lip. "I better not," I say. "I still hyperventilate every time I go anywhere."

And Father—*Ihmm-ihmm-ihmm-ihmmm!*—could be there.

Why would Father go to a soccer store? But I shiver thinking about it. Br-rr-rr!

Aaron slaps my shoulder—my good shoulder. "It's all right, Charlie. We'll go when you're up to it."

Mrs. H. and Aaron's mom come into the room. Mrs. Horowitz is pulling keys out of her purse, so I know the visit is over.

"I'm sorry you have to leave already," I say. Aaron's leaving makes me feel so sad. "But you'll come back?"

"Sure, Charlie. And you'll come see me when things get a little better."

"Yeah. Sure." When will that be?

From the front door, Mrs. H. and I watch Aaron and his mother leave. I feel worse and worse as they walk toward the curb and get into the car. Worse and worse as they ride away and disappear down the street.

I heave a sigh. "I wish I'd gone with him," I tell Mrs. H. "I really wish I'd gone."

Mrs. H. puts her arm around my shoulders and squeezes gently. The tricky place begins to hurt, but I don't care. "It will happen, Charlie," she says. "Give yourself time."

# CHAPTER TWENTY-SEVEN

I'm at the medical center again, waiting to see Dr. Leidy. I really wish she could come to Mrs. H.'s house.

Ambrose and Mrs. H. wait with me until Dr. Leidy comes out. They're going to shop for shoes. At breakfast Mrs. H. said they'd wait for me, and I could shop for shoes, too, but I said no. I hardly wear the ones I have. I'm used to going around in socks or barefoot, and besides, shoes pinch my toes. That's what I said.

Mrs. H. smiled. "Charlie," she answered, "that's why we buy new ones. You're outgrowing yours."

But I don't want to go. I just want to get Dr. Leidy's appointment over with and go home. Go where I can fold Mrs. H.'s walls around me like a soft, green blanket and be safe.

The basement where I lived with my parents rises around me. I wanted to hug those walls around me, too, when I was in the hospital, but they took those walls away. I never saw them again. Why did that have to happen? Because I locked myself out of the house. I have only myself to blame. But what would have happened if I hadn't locked myself out? Would I still be in the basement? Would I even be alive?

*Ihmm-ihmm-ihmm!* I shiver.

But Mrs. H.'s walls don't hold me like the basement's did, with hope inside me, wishing always for the kitchen door to open, wishing always that I can—could—live upstairs again.

That part's over. Mrs. H.'s walls hold me, though, in a place where no one hurts me, where I'm not hungry, and sometimes I get special food because Mrs. H. knows I like it. I am safe in Mrs. H.'s house, and I don't want to let go of that. Hope—I don't know. I'm afraid to hope too much.

I think about the split-pea soup with hot-dog chunks. My mother used to make that. Hers tasted different from Mrs. H.'s. Mother would sit and smile at me across the kitchen table, and we'd be quiet over the soup. And then I'd get out my papers and draw. Drawing so many hours, so many days.

Funny, but I haven't drawn a single picture since I came to Mrs. H.'s, not if you don't count what I've done for Mrs. West. I don't want to. And pictures were where I lived before all this happened.

There was that one picture I drew. I wish I could have that one back. A butterfly. Wide wings with a three-dot pattern on each one. The butterfly was flying high, over the grass, over the trees, near the clouds. The air was cool and clear and wonderful to fly through. I made the butterfly's back wide, and on that wide back, I drew a boy. Me. I flew with that butterfly through that cool, clear air up near the clouds. It made me so happy to work on that drawing. I worked on it for days, going so far and high on the back of that butterfly.

Then one day I couldn't find the drawing. I looked all over for it, but I never found it again. And I couldn't ask. Asking made Father angry.

I never could draw that picture again. I tried, but it never worked, somehow. No life in it. No life in me when I drew it.

"Charlie, Dr. Leidy called you."

I blink. For a moment, I thought I was in the kitchen with Mother and Father. But now the feeling is gone, gone like rain the next day.

I wave to Mrs. H. and Ambrose before following Dr. Leidy back to her office.

I know I'm all right with Mrs. H. and Ambrose. I know I'm all right with Dr. Leidy. It's just the space in between where anything can happen, *where they can get you!* But I walk it quickly against one bass's *ihmm*. Made it.

Inside her office I sit on the chair I always sit on, and Dr. Leidy says good morning with her wide smile while she takes the chair she always takes on the other side of the cloth-covered table. Today there's a truck with the blue and green cars, and one of the toy men has a beard like Father used to have. I pick him up.

"What's new, Charlie?" she asks.

I shrug with my good shoulder. "Not much. I didn't need to breathe into the bag when we got here this time. It was easier to breathe."

"I'm glad to hear that. Still sticking pretty close to the house, though?" she asks.

I put the toy man down and pick up the truck. This truck has doors that open with the edge of my fingernail. Open, close, open, close.

"I hate going outside. I hate big spaces. But I did run outside on Thanksgiving." I look up from the table and tell her about that. And I tell about feeling lousy because of missing Father and Mother.

For some reason it's easier to talk to Dr. Leidy today. I'm not sure why.

Yes. I feel safer. That's what it is. It's OK to talk. It doesn't matter if Father finds out what I say. I'm protected.

"Ambrose's brother stopped by," I said. "Ross. He was allowed. I wish my parents had been allowed, too. At least Mother. She won't hurt me."

"Suppose your mom had come. What would have happened then?"

"Oh, boy." I push the truck over to the man with the beard. Then I push the man with the beard against the truck to make it move. "I would have wanted to leave with her. Ambrose went out with Ross after dinner. They just drove around in Ross's car, driving and driving. Just having some time together. Maybe I could have done that with Mother. Just drive around for a while. And then come back to Mrs. H.'s house."

"Hmm." Dr. Leidy smiles at me. "You'd come back to Mrs. H.'s house?"

"What? Well—I'm supposed to—I mean, I'm living with Mrs. H. now."

"That's true."

What's Dr. Leidy thinking? I look at her for a clue, but her face tells me nothing. "Well, you know I can't go back home with Mother. That's—that's something that can't happen."

I think about the basement house. The lake house. Any house. No house is good. Not with Mother and Father. Not like it was once.

"You know what? I wouldn't even want to try it," I say.

"Why not?"

"I can't do that part again." I shake my head. Everything feels heavy.

"What part?"

So discouraged. "The basement part." I push a blue car against a green car and move the green car in a circle while I talk. "If I went with Mother, that's where I'd end up. She doesn't like it, but she can't save me from it. She can't stop Father. She can never stop Father."

And I feel the darkness of the basement, the patterns the sun made on the floor through the window well, the gray clothesline with its old clothespins. The furnace. So dark. *Ihmm-ma-ihmm-ma-ihmm* threads in and out of everything. All through me. If I could just get rid of that. *Ihmm-ma-ihmm-ma-ihmm* . . . I'm looking at the cars on the table, but I'm not really looking at them. The clothespins, the window well, the furnace. The basement. That's what I'm seeing.

"So now you would choose not to go with your mother. You would make that choice."

I shrug both shoulders. Ow! I can't always make myself remember. "I guess I would. I don't like it, but I would. I can't go back. Do you understand? I just can't go back to that." Tears jump into my eyes and spill down my cheeks. "I just can't."

"It's OK, Charlie. I understand." She pushes a box of tissues toward me.

I'm shaking my head. "Why does this have to be happening to me? Why can't it be made right?" I grab some tissues and wipe my eyes. So stupid. All of this.

*Ihmm-ma-ihmm-ma-ihmmm* . . . The spider basses pull me down to the dusty basement floor. There is no air, and all is hopeless. Nothing to be done.

"Listen, Charlie." Dr. Leidy's voice keeps a line for me from the basement to her office, and I hold on to it. "There are some things you can't do anything about."

"Right. Like the color of the sky."

"Yes. And that your parents put you in the basement."

"My father, not my mother."

"But there are things you can change."

"Like what?"

"You can do something about what happens next in your life. You can decide to stay locked in the basement in your mind, or you can step away from that. You can go forward. You can ask for things."

I consider what she's saying. "Ask for things?" This is a new idea. "Ask for things?" I stand up and circle the room, but it's not like the time I circled my chair three times and pulled on my ears. My eyebrows are almost up to my hairline. The basses play a high note, *screee!* They play high, then come apart like old string, and the basses are gone. Not just under the line. Not there. I feel a sense of wonder. "Ask for things? Me?"

And I think of split-pea soup with hot-dog chunks, orange soda with pizza. What else can I ask for? What else is there?

Dr. Leidy laughs. "What do you want?"

A million things *whir* through my head so fast I can't catch them. So many colors and sounds go by that I have to grab on to the back of my chair. Using two hands, I guide myself back to the seat.

"What I would like," I say, through all the rocking and whirling and clanging and colors, "is to go to a soccer game. To go to Aaron's soccer game."

Dr. Leidy reaches across the table to shake my hand. "That's wonderful, Charlie." Her grin lights her face. "Go for it."

## CHAPTER TWENTY-EIGHT

I'm going to walk Ambrose down to the bus stop. I don't want to, but I can't stay in the house if I'm going to figure out about getting to a soccer game. I have to push on the outside.

Besides, I love the outside. I remember that from before. When people come inside, they smell fresh. Their voices are different and excited. That's what the outside does. I want to have that, too.

The last time Father caught me outside, I was dancing in the rain. That rain felt so good! I loved the way the wind whipped through the trees and through my hair! Why wasn't I afraid that day? Then is when I had a reason to be afraid, but I wasn't. Well, I was, but not this way.

Ever since the hospital, I'm afraid to go outside. I'm not really sure why. Father isn't coming. He won't see me even if I stay outside all day. He can't do anything even if he does. Mrs. H. tells me that again and again, although I don't know why she's so sure.

I can feel Father. Every place I am—in the dining room, in the kitchen, standing at the window—I can feel Father watching me, like his face with that one slanted eyebrow is mixed up in the wallpaper. I feel him watching me and telling me to be quiet and to stay away from the windows and to only take one spoonful of sugar and not so much syrup, and put that orange juice *away*! I feel him warning me never to go outside. I feel him telling me—*Ihmmmm! Go down to the basement!* I can't go anywhere without that feeling.

When I think about going outside, I really feel him, and then I feel that basement—*Ihmmmmm!* with its crumbling walls and its old clothesline. *Ihmmmmm . . .*

Mrs. H. never sends me down to her basement. She understands.

"To tell you the truth," she told me one day while she was doing the wash in the laundry part of the kitchen, "I don't like the basement very much, myself. But that's the way basements are. All cold concrete and boxes and spiderwebs. Nothing scary, but not where you'd go for a treat, either."

"Here's the thing," I said. "Someday I'll be going back to Mother and Father. At least I think so. So I can't really forget all of Father's rules. Or forget about the basement."

"No," she said. "I guess you can't. That memory will stick with you your whole life. But you can decide not to follow those rules while you're with me. And you'll be surprised. By the time you're back with your parents, all the rules will be changed, the basement one, especially."

Hmm. Maybe. I don't see how.

"Well," I said, "how long do you think before I'm back living with Mother and Father?"

"Do you miss them?"

"Well . . ." I wasn't sure how to answer that. I miss them, but I don't, at the same time. "I just wonder how long I'll be living here."

She looked up at me from bending over the dryer door.

"Charlie, as far as I'm concerned, you can stay until you get married."

My laugh came out like a snort; that's such a funny idea. "Married? You mean, like, to a lady?"

"I sure don't mean to frogs." And she went back to pulling clothes out of the dryer—my green sweater and my other pair of blue jeans. It seems funny that she washes my clothes. But clean clothes feel so good after wearing those shorts for so long. She looked at me again. "Didn't Dr. Leidy tell you that you'll remain in foster care as long as you need it?" She hauled out some towels and the green pillowcase she uses to cover a throw pillow.

"Yes. But I want to go back to Father and Mother soon. I want safety and them."

"These things take time."

If I'm back with Father and Mother again . . . surely they want me back with them. And I want to be back with them, but . . .

*Ihmmmmm!* The basement.

That's where Father sent me when I did things wrong, like singing when he was working or smashing the sugar bowl on the kitchen floor. That white bowl with the pink flower shattered into so many pieces, and there was broken, white china mixed up with white sugar all over the kitchen floor. I would have cleaned it up, but Father's face got all red.

"Basement!" he roared. This was one time he wasn't quiet. He grabbed me by my arm—that was before I'd hurt my shoulder—and thrust me against the basement door. I opened it as fast as I could to get away from his hand, but not fast enough. One more push sent me flying, but I grabbed the banister, and that saved me from falling down the steps. *SLAM!* went the door behind me.

"Robert . . ." I could hear my mother's protest. "It was an accident. He didn't mean to—"

*Thump!*

"It's always an accident with you, isn't it?" thundered Father. "Always protecting the boy."

"He's a chil—"

*Thump!*

I hated those thumps.

"Now, you clean it up!"

I was glad I was in the basement. It was a safe place. I just wished I could have pulled Mother down with me as I went. It made me feel bad that there was nothing I could do to help her.

When Father said I could come up later, Mother had bruises on her cheeks, and she was limping. Her eyes were big and sad, but she shook her head at me, and I never heard a word about what happened while I was in the basement. It was easy to guess, but I didn't want to. I wanted to believe that those thumps were Father pounding his fist against the wall. He did that sometimes, and there were holes he made that way that Mother had to fix once in a while.

But when I came up, Mother did have bruises on her cheeks, and she was limping. I couldn't pretend those facts away.

Something I did ask Mother about one day, when Father was out jogging, was the sugar bowl. Because when I'd come up from the basement, it was in its place on the kitchen table again, just like I'd never been near it, and there wasn't so much as a stickiness on the blue tiles under my bare feet.

"Didn't I break that, Mother?" I was dusting an end table in the living room.

"Not that one," she answered over the cushion she was sewing on the sofa. She smiled at me. "I had an extra one in the closet in case it broke. I have a lot of extra things like that."

"But what if we break that one?"

"We will try not to," she said. She bit the thread to snap it from the cushion. "But just in case *Father* breaks it, I have two more."

I wondered about that. How many extras of things did Mother have tucked away? And how did she know she needed extra sugar bowls? But I didn't ask her.

*Push—Ouch!*—against my shoulder. Ambrose is here. But I don't say *ouch!*

"Hey, Charlie, aren't you coming?" Ambrose is wearing his coat and his backpack is in place. "I don't want to miss the bus."

Without wanting to, I grab my coat and head for the door with him. Mrs. H. walks outside with us. "Good for you, Charlie, good for you." She sits down on the front step. "Go on, Charlie. I'll be right here."

Ambrose is walking fast, and I have to hurry to keep up. I'm surprised how quickly we make it to the bus stop at the corner. It always looks so far away from the house. A bunch of the other kids are there ahead of us.

"This," says Ambrose with a wide, sweeping gesture, "is Charlie. He's my new big brother. Charlie, this is Rosie, Marianne, Blacky, and Fred."

Blacky's hair is so blond, it's almost white, so his name doesn't make any sense to me.

Rosie is talking. "So how old are you, Charlie?"

"Twelve."

"Are you going to the middle school?"

"Um, yes, I guess, sometime."

"When he's ready," puts in Ambrose. "Right, Charlie?"

Marianne throws some hair over a shoulder like Mrs. West does, only her hair is brown. "You're so lucky. You won't have to take the bus or anything, with only that field to walk across."

Only the field . . . *ihmmm* . . .

"They have a swimming pool at the middle school," says Blacky. "My sister says it's the coolest."

The bus makes the curve from the next street. "The bu-u-u-s!" yells everybody else together.

Why are they doing that? Then I see a girl with a ponytail on each side of her head fly out of the next house and run across the grass.

"That's Audrey," Ambrose tells me. "She misses the bus half the time." He lets Audrey, her half-open backpack slung over one shoulder, get in line ahead of him. She's eating a slice of jelly toast, and a smear of purple streaks her white shirt. Jelly's on her fingers, too, and on her cheeks. Sticky. Ick.

One at a time, all of the boys and girls climb into the bus. Ambrose turns around on the bottom step to wave at me.

Then he disappears farther inside. The door closes, and the bus roars up the street. So loud!

I'm alone. *Ihmmmmm!* Oh, no!

I have to get back to Mrs. H.'s house! I have to do it by myself! *Ihmm-ihmm-ihmm!* All this space between her house and me! I wish Ambrose was still here. Why did I think I could go back by myself? All this outside! *Ihmm-ihmm!*

Father's here. He must be; I feel him so strongly. *Ihmm-ihmm!*

Mrs. H. is still up there, sitting on the front step. She waves at me, and that makes me feel a little better. I wish she would come down and walk with me, but she's too far away to ask. *Ihmmmmm!* Twenty basses away.

"Run, Charlie! Run, run, run!" I hear that all the way up the street. My legs pump so hard. "Run, run, run." As I get to Mrs. H., I realize it's my own voice I hear tangling with— *Ihmmm! Ihmmmm!*—the basses.

"Good job," says Mrs. H.

I'm glad I'm here with Mrs. H. and glad I walked down to the bus stop and ran back. On my own.

"I went down to the bus stop," I tell Mrs. H. I know she knows it but I have to say it, anyway. Saying it makes it more real. "I went down to the bus stop with Ambrose, and I came back all by myself."

And what I'm thinking of is a soccer game. I'm going to get there.

# CHAPTER TWENTY-NINE

I'm kicking a soccer ball around the front yard while Mrs. H. finishes talking on the phone. We're going out to buy me some shoes. I wish Ambrose was here to play with, but he's at someone else's house this afternoon.

"As if you'd gone out to the soccer store with Aaron that day," explained Mrs. H., "just to have fun with a friend."

I understand, but I still like it better when Ambrose is here. Then I know where he is, and I don't have to worry.

Suddenly, there's a swarm of big kids on the sidewalk and the street. They're riding skateboards and scooters, like I've seen other kids ride since I've lived here with Mrs. H. and Ambrose. But these are big kids—a whole bunch of them at once—hooting and laughing, like the big kids at the lake house that time. I make a run for the house—*If they see you, they can get you!*—but Mrs. H. is there, locking the door behind her.

"Let me in; let me in!" I shout.

She looks at me surprised. "What's the matter?" she says. "Did you change your mind about the shoes?"

But before I can answer, all those big kids are up on the lawn, coming up the walk, and Mrs. H. and I are surrounded.

"Mrs. Harrigan, Mrs. Harrigan," they're shouting.

Their faces are red and big and everywhere. I press up against the door behind Mrs. H.

*Big kids, big kids!*

"What is it, boys?" Mrs. H. asks. Her voice is calm.

They're all answering at once, but I can't understand anything. And why isn't Mrs. H. afraid? They're going to get us. They'll hurt us and we'll be—

*—yanked in my red wagon—Bump! Bump! Bump!—over the rocks right to the water. SPLASH! "Ha-ha-ha-ha!"*

"Look, Charlie," says Mrs. H. She's holding a photograph under my eyes. I still see the big kids at the lake on their bikes, so at first I can't figure out what I'm looking at. Then I can. It's a baby, even smaller than Clarice.

I still don't understand.

"Their mother had a baby this morning," Mrs. H. tells me. "A little girl. Isn't that great? All those boys and now a little girl."

"Her name's Daisy," puts in one of the big kids. "Daisy Mae."

I feel sick, but I make myself smile.

Mrs. H. hands the photograph back to the biggest big kid. Actually I'm thinking some of those big kids aren't any taller than I am. One can't be any bigger than Ambrose. But they were acting like—

"Tell your dad I'll send over a casserole," Mrs. H. tells the big kids.

And all those big kids leave, some on skateboards, some on scooters, a couple on foot. I hadn't noticed the runners before. They start down the street again, laughing and hooting like before. A couple of houses down, they stop again to show the mailman the picture.

"Some of those boys are cousins," Mrs. H. remarks. "Polly didn't have *all* of them. But still. A little girl among all those boys. No wonder they're so excited."

They didn't get us. We're all right. I sink onto the doormat and try to get my breath. We're all right.

Mrs. H. looks down at me. "Why, Charlie, what's the matter?"

"Big kids," I gasp. "I thought they were going to hurt us."

"Why?" She sits on the mat next to me and puts a gentle arm around my shoulder.

"Big kids—if they see you, they can get you."

"What?"

So I tell her about what happened at the lake house—how those big kids came up on bikes when I was playing and yanked me down to the lake in my wagon. How I bounced so high when the wheels hit the rocks, how the big kids dumped me into the water, how they laughed and hooted the whole time, and how scared I was.

"That's just terrible," says Mrs. H. "What did your parents do about it?"

"After the police left, Mother and I sat in the house watching Father walk and walk around the lake. That's what Father does when he's upset—walk. I'm always making him walk."

Mrs. H. rocks me gently from side to side. "No, you're not," she said. "That's his decision."

"But when he came back, he said we had to leave the lake. Those big kids ruined everything for us, he said, and then we moved to the basement house. Father was right."

"About what?"

"That what they did ruined me. It turned me into a bad kid. No matter how hard I tried after that, it turned me into a bad kid."

"No, it didn't."

"But it did. Father said so."

We sit on that cold doormat for a little longer. Then Mrs. H. stands up. She pulls me up with her.

"Come on, Charlie," she says. "I want to go buy a pair of shoes for a super kid."

I have to think about what she says for a minute. "Oh, you mean me!"

"I mean you," she says. "A super, super kid, and don't you ever forget it."

# CHAPTER THIRTY

A man called Mr. Carter is here at Mrs. H.'s to talk to me about what happened in the basement house. I don't want to talk to him. I sit on the sofa next to Mrs. H. while he asks questions, but I never say anything. What I'm really doing is putting myself somewhere else, somewhere deep inside my head. It's quiet here, and the colors are soft. Oh! The butterfly I drew a long time ago is here. I ride the butterfly far, far away, so I can hardly hear Mr. Carter's questions.

"Did your father ever hit you?"

Over the woods, under the bluest sky, feel the wind!

"Did your father ever lock you in the basement?"

To the lake with the waterbirds overhead! Smell the beech trees in the soft rain! Wind and rain and leaves are everything! I ride high. Higher and higher away so even the cries of the loon can't reach me.

"How many nights were you in the basement?" But oh-h-h Mr. Carter's words can. "How many?"

Down, down the butterfly falls, pulled by his heavy voice.

Every night
twilight.
Skip a few.
I love you.

"Charlie, please answer." Stern and heavy.

Then the butterfly drops away so I can't see it anymore. The basses pull me down so fast, I'm dizzy and my stomach hurts. The basement floor holds me. It doesn't matter that Mrs. H. is sitting next to me on her living-room sofa; this is the basement. The gray clothesline with the gray clothespins hangs where it's always hung. The steps lead up, and the window well slants the sun across the floor. Spider basses fill my ears and reach back into my bad shoulder and down to my stomach. Everything in between is buzzing with the *ihmms*. Yes, yes, this is the basement.

"Charlie?"

Oh, Father! Mother! Help!! *Ihmmmm! Ihmmmmm!*

"Mr. Carter." It's Mrs. H.'s voice. I'm so glad to hear her voice! She won't let anything bad happen. She'll protect me. I sniff the air to catch the faint floweriness of her hair. Mrs. H. loves me. "Mr. Carter, that's enough. Surely you can see that Charlie can't help the court case, yet."

I don't say anything the whole time, just stare at the fading blue jeans I'm wearing that Mrs. H. bought for me. I'm quiet and still, wishing myself away, wishing the basses would go away.

Something nudges my good shoulder. I don't look up.

"Mr. Carter is gone," Mrs. H. says. "Are you all right?"

I don't answer. I stay where I am, quiet and still. Oh, basement, basement, comfort me!

I don't move until the day is dark. Then I crawl silently up the stairs to listen at the door. Father is only on the other side of it. Can he hear me like I can hear him? Does he feel that uncuttable line between his chest and mine?

But the door at the top of the basement stairs is open, and my bed is what I see, not the kitchen with Father working at his desk. My bed in Mrs. H.'s house. In MY house, where I live, NOT the basement! Wake up, Charlie! You are OK. You are protected from the basement!

I come back downstairs to find Mrs. H. She's standing in the middle of the living room, worry all over her face.

"I'm so thirsty," I say. "Could I have some water? Water without ice?"

"Why, certainly, Charlie," and the worried look fades.

I follow her to the kitchen.

"All OK, now?" she asks. "What happened?"

"I'm not sure. But I'm fine now."

# CHAPTER THIRTY-ONE

"Time for lunch?" Ambrose asks. Mrs. H. has opened the kitchen door and stepped out into the January air to watch us in the backyard.

Ambrose kicks the soccer ball past me. I chase it and kick it back.

"Almost," she answers. She comes down the steps, and I see her pocketbook slung over her shoulder. "I have to run to the store for a couple of minutes, guys. Do you want to come or do you want to stay?"

"Oh, we'll be all right," says Ambrose. "Charlie's twelve, you know."

Twelve. What's that mean? That I'm old enough, supposedly, for something. Old enough to stay here with Ambrose while Mrs. H. goes out.

"OK, Charlie?" asks Mrs. H. "I'll only be gone fifteen minutes or so."

I bite my lower lip and look around. I'm safe in this backyard, right? And I can go into the house anytime I want, right? And it's safe there, right?

So I say yes. "That's fine," I say. Fifteen minutes. I can push the boundaries through fifteen minutes.

Mrs. H. disappears around the side of the house, and in a short time, we hear her car start up. Then that sound fades, and we know she's on her way.

"Come on, Charlie," says Ambrose. "Come on."

"What?" I look down. I'm holding the ball.

I throw it and we start to run again, kicking at the ball and banging into each other with Ambrose laughing the whole time. Sometimes I don't care what it is we're doing as long as Ambrose is laughing. His laugh makes me laugh, too.

Kick, laugh, run, run, kick, kick, laugh, WHOOPS! We slip on that muddy spot next to the garden. We get up, giggling. I point to Ambrose's muddy legs, and he points, laughing even harder, to the mud dripping from my arms. Then something is different and his face changes. I look to the corner of the house to see wha—

FATHER!

Laughter freezes in the air, and I back into Ambrose. He's not laughing anymore, either, and he holds me hard on the arm. How does he know? He's never seen Father.

"Hello, Charlie." Father steps farther into the backyard. He looks at me, taking in my muddy arms. He doesn't say anything about the mess, but I know he doesn't like it. Why do I have to be a mess the moment he's here? But what's he doing here? I thought he wasn't supposed to come.

"Hello, Father." My teeth are chattering, and Ambrose is looking up at me. *IHMMMMM!* A hundred basses fill the air. A hundred hundred.

"Are you well?" Father's voice is soft.

"Yes." *IHMMMMM!*

"We'll be seeing each other at the courthouse next week." Still soft, and he stops walking, both brown shoes pointing at me from the same invisible line.

*IHMMMMM . . .*

"What are you going to say, Charlie?"

I open my mouth, but I don't answer. How can I with more and more spider basses crowding my head?

"Charlie?" Father advances a couple of steps closer.

"Let's get out of here," whispers Ambrose. He tugs on my sleeve, but my feet are stuck, frozen, to the ground. "Run!" I can't move, not even to blink my eyes, staring at Father. Ambrose drops my arm and tears up the concrete steps into the house. "Mrs. H.! Mrs. H.!" he shouts. He's forgotten that Mrs. H. is at the store.

"Mother and I love you," Father says. "We'd never hurt you. We protected you. We kept you safe."

From who? But I don't ask.

Ambrose has left the back door open, so I hear the squeak of Mrs. H.'s basement door opening in the kitchen. "Mrs. H.! Mrs. H.!" Ambrose's voice is muffled. "Mrs. H.!"

"Father . . ." I'm so conscious of my arms, my dirty, messy arms. I feel dirty all over. My throat swells up inside, and tears roll down my cheeks. Dirty.

"Don't you know we love you?" His voice is still soft. So quiet. I'm so scared of his soft, quiet voice. "Of course we love you." *IHMMMMM . . .*

I make myself talk. Somehow I believe this will be my only chance. "Father, why? Why did you lock me in the basement? How could you do that to me?"

"Mrs. H.!" I can tell by the way Ambrose's voice echoes that he is standing outside on the front steps.

OUTSIDE! But the outside is here. Father is here. The

basement is here. It's all here, right in Mrs. H.'s backyard, with each bush and tree absolutely throbbing with every single brown, spider bass in the whole world.

*IHMMMMM! IHMMMMM! IHMMMMM!*

Father steps a little nearer. I am so scared. I can't move, with all the basses. They start with Father and end with me. I'm attached to him by the basses, like a rope tight between us. The invisible but uncuttable line that has always tied us together. Like in the basement. Like at the lake house. Like here. Anywhere. Always. *IHMMMMM! IHMMMMM!* The rope is so tight!

"We were protecting you." Father makes a sudden movement. I flinch, but he doesn't hit me. "I am not a violent man," he says, because I flinched. "I am quiet; that's all. I keep to myself. I don't hurt people. I certainly don't hit *little boys*."

"Father." Where is Ambrose? And shouldn't Mrs. H. be back by now? "Do you really love me?" It's all I've ever cared about.

"Of course."

Oh, that feels so good to hear. I close my eyes and feel the goodness of it. That's all I want. That's all that any of this has ever been about. Does he love me? Yes. He loves me.

He loves me.

Father goes on. "Why else do you think we worked so hard to protect you—to keep you safe? That's why we lived away from people at the lake house; that's why we kept you inside in the house in town; that's why we sent you to the basement. Because we love you."

He and Mother were protecting me.

"Is that why we didn't have Christmas and Thanksgiving? Or Halloween and birthdays? To protect me? Is that the same reason?"

"Christmas!" He spits the word like it's poison in his mouth. "Christmas! That one's the worst of all of them. Those days are lies, promising some kind of special love that doesn't even exist. Huh! Lies! Fairy tales! We protected you from all those things so you would learn to be a good person and not end up bad like all those other kids."

All of them? But I'm thinking of Daisy's brothers. They weren't bad. I thought they were, but they weren't. And how could sending me to the basement be protecting me or helping me learn to be good?

Father looks around the yard, then jerks his dark eyes back to mine. "Now, listen, Charlie. You have to tell them the good stuff when you go to court next week. That we took care of you, that we never hurt you. You tell them that you made up all the bad stuff because you were sick. That's the truth. The spider and the basement and everything. After that, we'll live together just like before. You, Mother, and me."

Just like before? Dr. Leidy says he can't make that happen. Mrs. H. says that, too. Are they wrong and he's right? Does he know something they don't know? Will I live with Mother and Father just like before?

The basement's gritty walls crush me. I can't breathe! I can't breathe!

*IHMMMMM! IHMMMMM!*

Something from way inside my gut makes me force it out. "No!"

"Charlie!" Father's face is suddenly deep red like the spider, and he's lost his temper. "Ungrateful kid." He takes another step toward me. "*Ruined!* I knew it. Ever since those kids came by the lake house, no matter what we did, you were contaminated. Ruined."

Suddenly his hands are around my neck, and he's shaking me. I reach my hands out, but his arms are moving so fast, I can't get a grip on him. He's shaking and shaking me. My head is flopping around and so are my arms.

Footsteps sound behind me, and Ambrose shrieks. "Mrs. H.! Mrs. H.!"

Father lets go, and I fall awkwardly to the ground. *SNAP!* goes that spot in my bad shoulder that all those other falls and bumps have missed. *SNAP! CRACK!* White lightning's all around with *IHMMM*s mixing through, but I can still hear.

"Now, you listen to me!"

"Charlie, what was that noise?" Ambrose asks under Father's words.

"I'm your father, and that's *it!*"

"I can't find Mrs. H."

"*It!*"

"What was that noise, Charlie? What was it?"

Carefully, I stand up. Ambrose puts himself between Father and me. His head presses against my stomach. I cross my good arm over Ambrose's head to hold my bad arm by the elbow so it doesn't pull on the shoulder any more than it has to. So I can keep down the white lightning.

Father is standing there, looking at me while Ambrose pushes against me with his head, chin tilted toward Father, and I'm holding my elbow while the white lightning flashes on and off.

"Come on, Charlie." Father's voice has changed. It's quiet and pleasant sounding, the way I like to hear it. "Come with me. A son's place is with his father and mother." Sweet like sugared molasses. "Don't you want to live with Mother and me? You know we love you. We would never hurt you. Never have and never will. We'll have spaghetti with Italian bread. We'll have it tonight."

*Ihmmm.* The basses are dimming. Ten basses.

"Spaghetti and meatballs?" I breathe. I love Italian bread. That means I'll be upstairs. But he said I made up the basement, same as the spider. He said I was ruined.

"Sure. With meatballs. Come with me. Mrs. Harrigan won't mind if you come with me for dinner. What would be wrong with that—a boy home with his parents for dinner?" Now Father's voice soothes like a warm blanket all around me. Feels so good. *Ihmm.* Five basses. I can relax right into this. It's good. All good. Father does love me. I hear it in the honey of his voice. "No basement or any of that other stuff," he says. "We'll be back together and everything will be fine."

*Ihm.* One bass. Ah-h-h. Feels so good.

No basses. Clean and warm. Ah-h-h. Relax into the good. Just good. But good.

I'm falling into that warm blanket. Sure. I'll do what he wants. I'll come with him, and life will be good again. He says so. My shoulder will be fine. Everything will be fine. As soon as the white lightning goes away.

I push Ambrose's head with my hip so I can move around him and get closer to Father. Closer, closer.

Ambrose looks up at me with his mouth wide open, but I can't worry about that right now.

Closer, closer.

Ambrose throws his arms around my legs, jolting my shoulder and making the white lightning flare bright again. I stop, gasping. "It's bad to kick your children down the stairs in the dark," he says to me, and there's no laughing in his voice. None. Not even hiding-like. "It's bad every time," he adds, and his voice is serious all through. "Even if they wet the bed, even if they break the dishes, even if they laugh too loud. Charliecharliecharlie, don't you see?"

"Let him go, kid," says Father.

I look down at my brother. Every motion shocks me with the white lightning. Strange how its light makes Ambrose's words so clear. "You really miss your mother, don't you, Ambrose?"

He nods. "But she was bad to hurt me. She was, Charlie."

"Yes." I'm dizzy, and my stomach churns with lightning jabs. I look at Father. "She was," I tell him. "She was."

"What are you talking about? Come on, Charlie; come with me." He reaches out for a hand, but I'm holding on to Ambrose with the only good one I have. I'm holding him tight. Even if I wanted to give Father the other one, it could only hang from an arm and a twice-broken shoulder. It's no good. "You belong to your mother and me."

I realize I have no hands I can ever give him.

The kitchen door opens wide from how Ambrose left it,

and there is Mrs. H. "Oh, my God!" Clutching a wooden spoon in one hand, she runs down the steps. "Get out, get out, get out!"

"Now, Mrs. Harrigan," begins Father, his voice all smoothness and honey. "I only came to see my boy."

"Get out, get out, get out!"

"Where were you?" asks Ambrose. "I tried to find you."

"It's not so terrible for a father to want to see his son, is it?" Father continues.

He said I was ruined.

Mrs. H. has Father by the arm and is yanking him away.

"Wait, Mrs. H.," I say over Ambrose's head. "I need to say something to Father."

She pauses, tight-faced, her hand still on Father's arm. "Go on, Charlie," she says. Cold air blows through the backyard. I think it's cold. Wasn't it already cold out here? Out in the outside? I know it's cold out here. It has to be cold out here, but why don't I feel it?

"Father," I say. How can words I say sound like I'm saying them from so far away? "I will tell the truth in court. I will say you kept me in the basement. Because—*you*—*did*. And—I am *not* ruined. I am *not*!"

Father's face is red. "Why, you—"

"Is that all you need to say, Charlie?" interrupts Mrs. H.

"That's all."

Mrs. H. moves fast. She has Father around the side of the house before he can say another word. "You better do what I said, Charlie," he hollers. "I'm your *father*." Then—"You *better!*" His shout is farther away.

"He's on the walk," says Ambrose. "You can tell by the echo."

I nod even though I think every sound is coming from far away. Far away and frozen like an ice cube.

"You just better!" Even farther. The curb, I think.

That's the last, though. I hear a car start up, and I figure it's Father's. Mean, sick Father's.

Ambrose and I don't move until we see Mrs. H. round the corner of the house again. "He's gone, Charlie; he's gone."

"Are you sure?" I ask.

"Surer than sure."

Ambrose finally lets go and steps away. He and I look at each other. Both of us are shaking our heads.

"Were you really gonna go with him?" Ambrose asks.

"I don't know," I answer. The hum of the basses fills my ears. I swallow to make it go away, but it doesn't. "Maybe. Until you stopped me. Thanks."

Mrs. H. is with Ambrose and me now at the foot of the steps. She runs her fingers through my crew cut, then through Ambrose's hair. She hugs both of us real tight. I hear a mild thud through the white lightning, and I know she's dropped the wooden spoon onto the grass.

"Did you hit him with that?" asks Ambrose.

Mrs. H. lets go of us and collapses onto the middle of the steps. "You know what, guys?" she asks. "I forgot I was even holding it." She wipes her eyes. "I should never have left you alone," she says. "I'm so sorry."

I heave a huge sigh and sit carefully on the step below Mrs. H.'s. The flowery smell in her hair covers the *ihmm*s and makes them fall apart. It feels like ice turning into water real fast.

Ambrose sits next to Mrs. H. Mrs. H. and Ambrose and me together. So good.

No more basement for me. I know that now for sure.

I lean against the wall beside me; the hard, firm wall; a wall I can count on. "Mrs. H.," I say, "my shoulder's bad."

# CHAPTER THIRTY-TWO

"I'm home from my shoulder surgery, Aaron."

"How's it feel?"

I pause. "You know what? The doctor had to break some bones to really fix things, but I already feel better. Still hurts, but it feels better. The doctor told me that would happen. He said after it heals, I can play soccer if I want. I asked him."

"That's great, Charlie."

"How's *your* arm?"

"Fine. I've been practicing a little with the guys. Just pickup stuff, but soon I'll be back in the goal with the team. How's the outside problem doing?"

"I'm still working on it. Ever since my father came to the house, I had to almost start over again on that. But I'll walk a little farther outside every day. I'll get there."

"Maybe you'll be able to see a soccer game soon."

"Pretty soon, Aaron. I'm sure of it."

CHAPTER THIRTY-THREE

It's February fifteenth, and I'm walking with Mrs. H. and Ambrose around a soccer field a long way from home. The ground is wet, and I'm being real careful not to slip because of my shoulder. I'm still using a sling.

I don't feel real good being outside, so far from the car, so far from Mrs. H.'s house—my house. But I've decided I can do this. I feel good enough. Only five basses—*ihmm*—follow me.

Then I see it. "A fight!" I grab Mrs. H.'s arm. "A fight!" I feel so awful watching the knot of violence on the field. "They're hurting each other! They're hurting each other!"

"No, they're not," says Mrs. H. Her voice is calm, and she keeps on walking. "That's just a bunch of guys sliding and falling over the ball."

"Oh." I see the players disconnect and run, except for two that slip and splash onto their faces again.

Because the field is muddy after the rain of the last three days. But Aaron said to come, anyway. "What's a little mud?" If this is a little mud, what's a lot?

We go past the net on one side, and I see that Aaron's inside it. He's wearing a puffy, striped shirt and long, black pants—at least the part of him I can see that isn't brown with mud. He's standing between the net and a huge puddle. "Hey, Aaron," I shout.

He turns his head. A streak of mud runs from one eye to his chin. "Well, look who's here."

Ambrose, Mrs. H., and I keep going until we reach the seats. Mrs. H. calls them bleachers. Some people, parents, I'm guessing, are there ahead of us. One of them is Aaron's dad.

"Hey, Charlie," he says to me. "How are you doing?"

"Fine." I introduce him to Mrs. H. and Ambrose. "We finally got to a game."

We settle in to watch. Some of the parents are screaming instructions to their sons.

"Up the side, Bobby; up the side!"

"Pass it, Romeo. *Romeo, pass it!*"

"Shoot, shoot, shoot!"

All the screaming makes me scared and nervous, but Mrs. H. seems calm. Ambrose seems calm. I guess it's all right, but I don't like it.

Mrs. H. looks at me and pats the hand on my good side. I know she'd squeeze my shoulders if I hadn't had the surgery. Knowing that helps.

I don't know what all the screaming means, so I just watch. I figure that if there's anything wrong, Mrs. H. or Aaron's dad will tell us.

Here comes the ball. One player's way ahead of everyone else, kicking the ball and splashing with every step. Every time the ball bounces, water shoots up.

"Breakaway!" shouts Aaron's dad. He stands up, holding his mug of coffee, but he doesn't shout anymore. He just watches Aaron.

So do I. Aaron leaps just as the opposing player kicks the ball. Aaron sails through the air, arms wide, and knocks the ball to the ground. It splashes in the big puddle and so does Aaron. He falls into it, in fact, and hugs the ball.

"Great save!" shouts Mr. Horowitz.

Aaron smiles and throws the ball down the field. The running and yelling begin again. I look at Aaron. Mud's dripping from his hair and down his shirt and from his elbows. He's soaked with mud. I look at Aaron's dad, who's all proud. Lucky Aaron.

Then I look at Mrs. H. and Ambrose, and I think, lucky me.

Before the end of the game, all of the boys are so muddy that I don't know how they can tell which players are on which team, but they sure look like they're having fun. When, after a long time, we hear three long toots on a whistle, the action stops. The boys trail off the field.

"The game is over," Mrs. H. tells me.

The teams line up to face then pass each other.

"Good game."

"Good game."

"Good game."

"Good game."

Then Aaron comes to join us in the bleachers, and right there, on this raw February day, he pulls off his shirt and tosses it onto the grass. I laugh because even his skin got muddy through his shirt. His father gives him a towel and then a clean shirt. Then a jacket.

"So, Charlie," Aaron says. "You made it."

"Yup. I made it."

A man wearing a green jacket and hat approaches the bleachers. He's carrying some flat white boxes. "Someone here call for pizza? Pizza and soda?"

And that pizza is so good with the orange soda.

# CHAPTER THIRTY-FOUR

The court date's been postponed and postponed and postponed since Father came to Mrs. H.'s house. Now it's early March, and I'm waiting with Ellis in a hallway outside the courtroom.

Mr. Carter might call me in to testify. Mother has promised to tell everything. That's what Mr. Carter said this morning, so he thinks maybe he won't need me. But I'm here. Just in case. Just in case what, I'm not sure, but I'm here.

I was in the courtroom for a few minutes, but the judge said I could wait in the hall after things got started. He asked Mother and Father first if it was fine with them if I wasn't right in the room. I could be called back anytime, he told them. So I was allowed to leave. I don't want to be in there, but I don't like waiting here much, either.

Ellis is trying to distract me by reading *The Adventures of Huckleberry Finn* out loud while we wait, but it's hard to listen, and it's hard to sit.

What's going on in the courtroom? Is Mother really telling everything with Father right there listening? How can she do that? He might hit her.

Is Mrs. H. telling them what Father said at her house? Is Ambrose telling them how he saw Father's hands around my neck? What's going on?

Will Father go to prison? Will Mother?

I wish this day was yesterday. I wish I didn't have to sit here not knowing. I wish lots of things.

I'm asking Ellis for the hundredth time if he thinks they'll call me, when the door to the courtroom opens and a rush of people seem to fall out of it.

The first person I see is Mother. She runs to me, and I run to her. She hugs me. "Oh, Charlie," she says.

"What happened?" I ask.

Then I see Father. His face isn't red or even pink. It's a dead white. And he's really skinny. He doesn't stop walking. He does look at me with Mother, but it's with an empty face, like he doesn't know us.

Then Mother says, "I love you, Charlie." She buttons a coat around her. It's one I've never seen before, and it's lighter, I think, so she can stand up straighter under it. "This is going to work out," she says. "We'll be together again."

She kisses my cheek, and I kiss hers. Then she leaves, waving at me from the courthouse door. She looks tired, but she's smiling, so I'm thinking maybe she's right. Things will work out.

Mr. Carter is with Mrs. H., and Ambrose is holding her hand. The grown-ups are talking with Ellis, and everyone is smiling.

"What happened?" I ask.

"They were convicted," says Mrs. H.

Convicted? That doesn't make me smile.

"We'll be asking for probation for your mother," says Mr. Carter. "That means she won't have to go to jail. She told everything that happened. She wanted to tell. You could see that."

I nod. "What about Father?"

"I think he'll be sent to a place for sick people. A mental hospital for criminals. That's what we'll ask for. Of course, there will undoubtedly be appeals, so all this may take a while. Years, probably."

"Years?" I look at Mrs. H. "Will I get to see Mother?"

Mrs. H. nods. "Maybe. We'll see how it all works out."

THIRTY-FIVE

---

Snow! I haven't touched snow since the lake house, and when I wake up this Sunday morning, it's coming out of the sky.

"Come on, Charlie," Ambrose says. We haven't even had breakfast, and Ambrose already has his coat on. "The first real snow of the year! I've been waiting all winter for this. Maybe we'll get a snowstorm! Maybe I'll get a snow day from school tomorrow! *Maybe!*"

I laugh, and then I look at Mrs. H.

"Go ahead," she says, smiling at me. "Just be careful not to slip and hurt that shoulder."

"Aw, there's nothing to slip *on* yet," says Ambrose. "You can still see all the grass."

I go outside with Ambrose. Because of my sling, my coat only hangs over that shoulder.

The crisp air makes my eyes water, and the snow is soft like a kiss on my face. I turn my face into the kisses that makes the snow feel warm.

"Taste one," says Ambrose.

I look at him. His mouth is open, and his tongue is stuck out. I do the same, and—whoa! that snow is *cold!*

Ambrose and I walk across the street to the soccer field. No one's playing soccer this morning, and I think about Aaron's game. It looked like fun, and I'd like to learn how to play.

I follow Ambrose past the soccer field and around the school to where there's a bunch of trees. I turn around. I can't see Mrs. H.'s house from here. I think about how that feels. My heart's not beating hard, my breath is OK. I don't feel scared at all. Only two *ihm*s if I think about them. Or one. Maybe none for real, someday. I touch the cold, rough bark of one of the trees. I love this tree, and it loves me. I can feel it.

The air is so—so—I don't know the word. I feel GOOD! It's great to be outside with my eyes watering in the snowy brightness. I can't help it. I circle and circle with my good arm extended. In a minute, I'm going to jump as high and holler as loud as I can.

I grin at Ambrose. He grins back. "Oh, Charlie," he says, and I know just what he means. "Oh, Charlie."

Then I shout.

"YAHOO!"

He shouts with me.

"YAHOO! YAHOO!"

Me and my brother—we're going to shout forever!